GREEN LANTERN
THE ANIMATED SERIES™

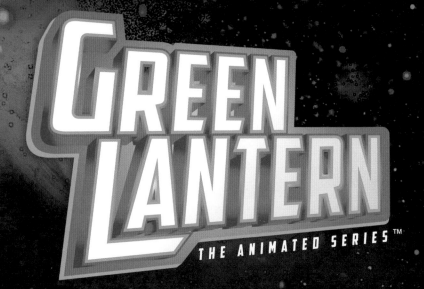

STONE ARCH BOOKS
a capstone imprint

STONE ARCH BOOKS™
Published in 2014
A Capstone Imprint
1710 Roe Crest Drive
North Mankato, MN 56003
www.capstonepub.com

DC Comics
1700 Broadway, New York, NY 10019
A Warner Bros. Entertainment Company

Cataloging-in-Publication Data is available at the
Library of Congress website:
ISBN: 978-1-4342-4787-2 (library binding)

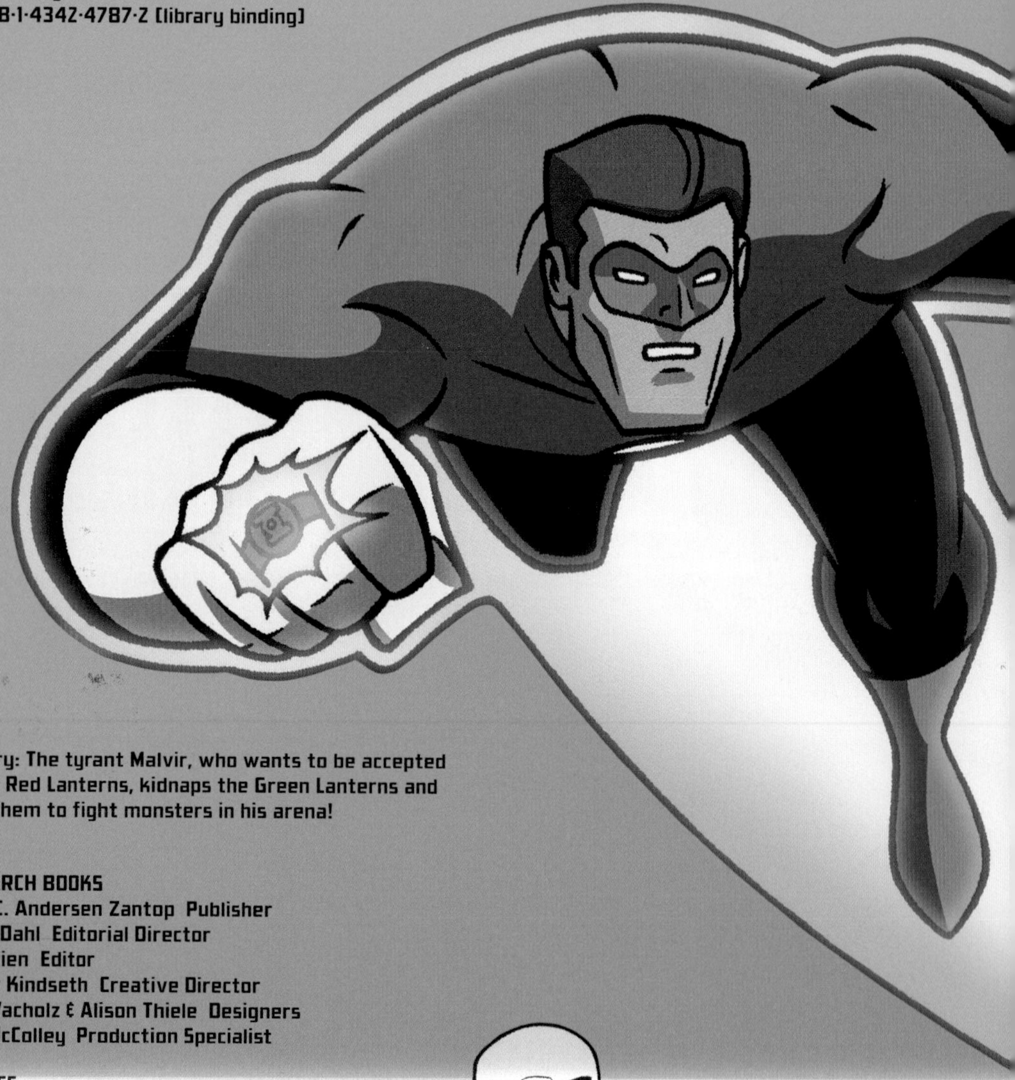

Summary: The tyrant Malvir, who wants to be accepted into the Red Lanterns, kidnaps the Green Lanterns and forces them to fight monsters in his arena!

STONE ARCH BOOKS
Ashley C. Andersen Zantop Publisher
Michael Dahl Editorial Director
Sean Tulien Editor
Heather Kindseth Creative Director
Hilary Wacholz & Alison Thiele Designers
Kathy McColley Production Specialist

DC COMICS
Kristy Quinn Original U.S. Editor

Printed in the United States of America
in Stevens Point, Wisconsin.
062014 008322R

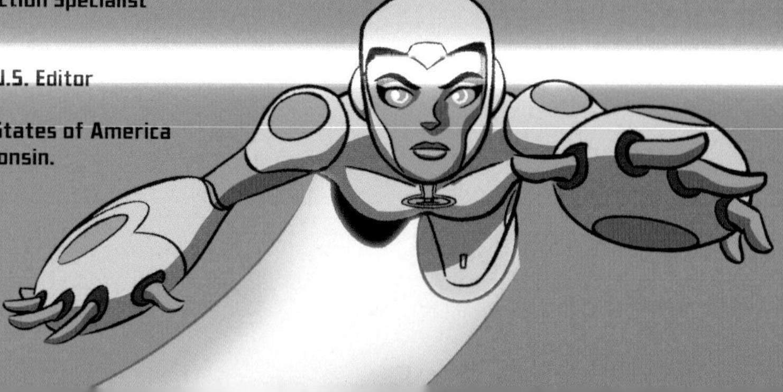

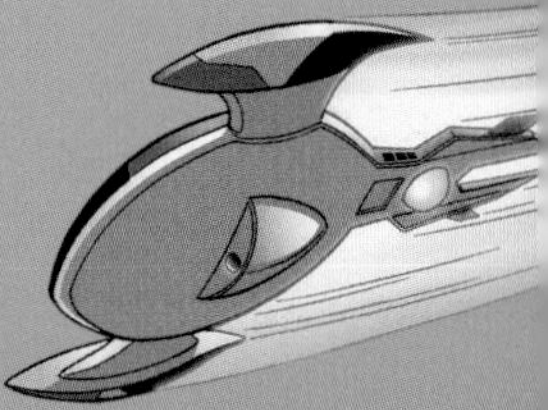

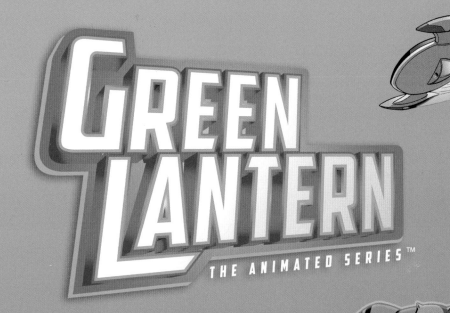

GREEN LANTERN

THE ANIMATED SERIES™

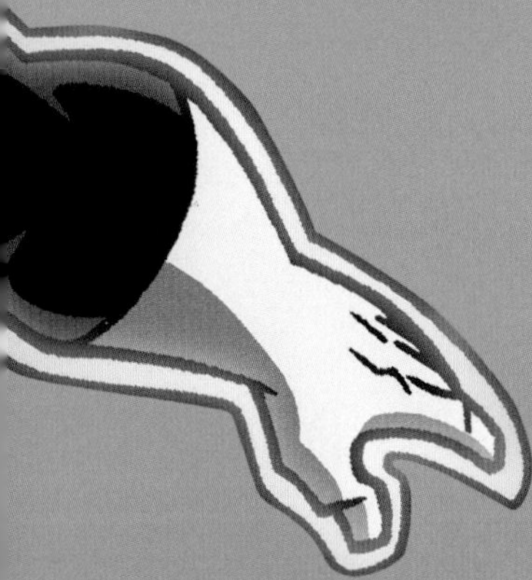

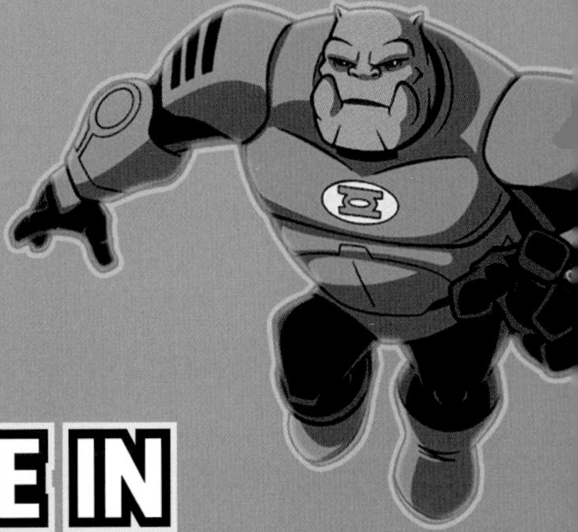

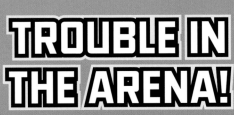

TROUBLE IN THE ARENA!

Art Baltazar & Franco....................writers
Dario Brizuela........................... illustrator
Gabe Eltaeb ....colorist
Saida Temofonte ....letterer

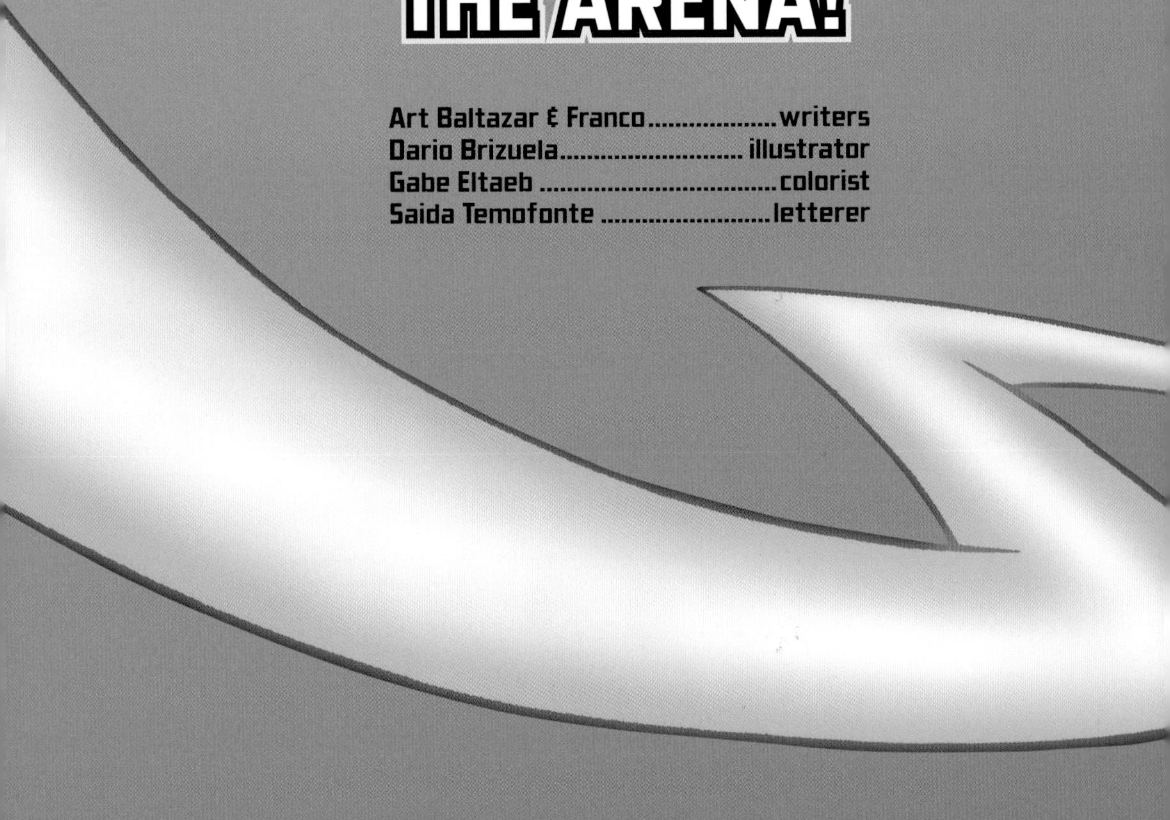

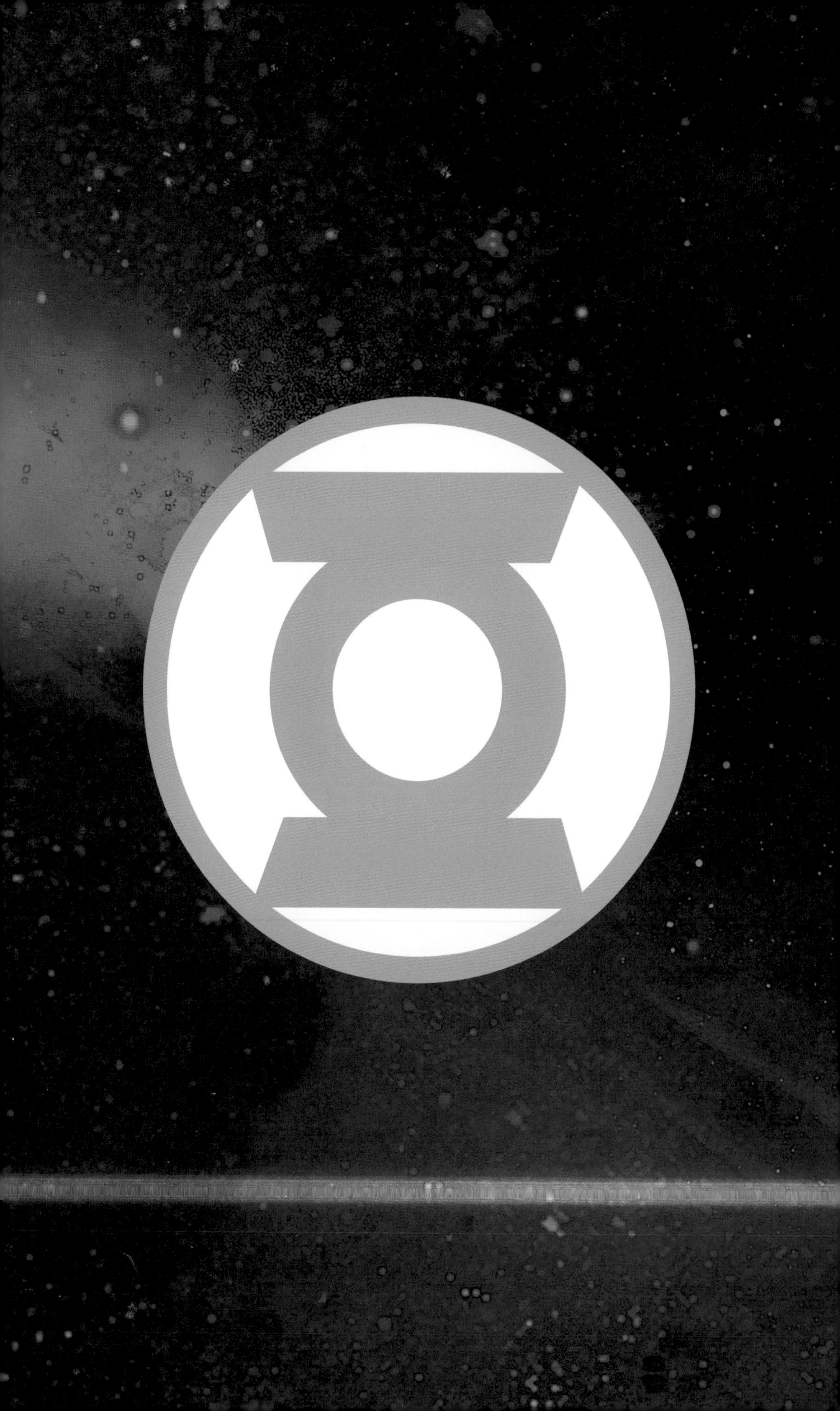

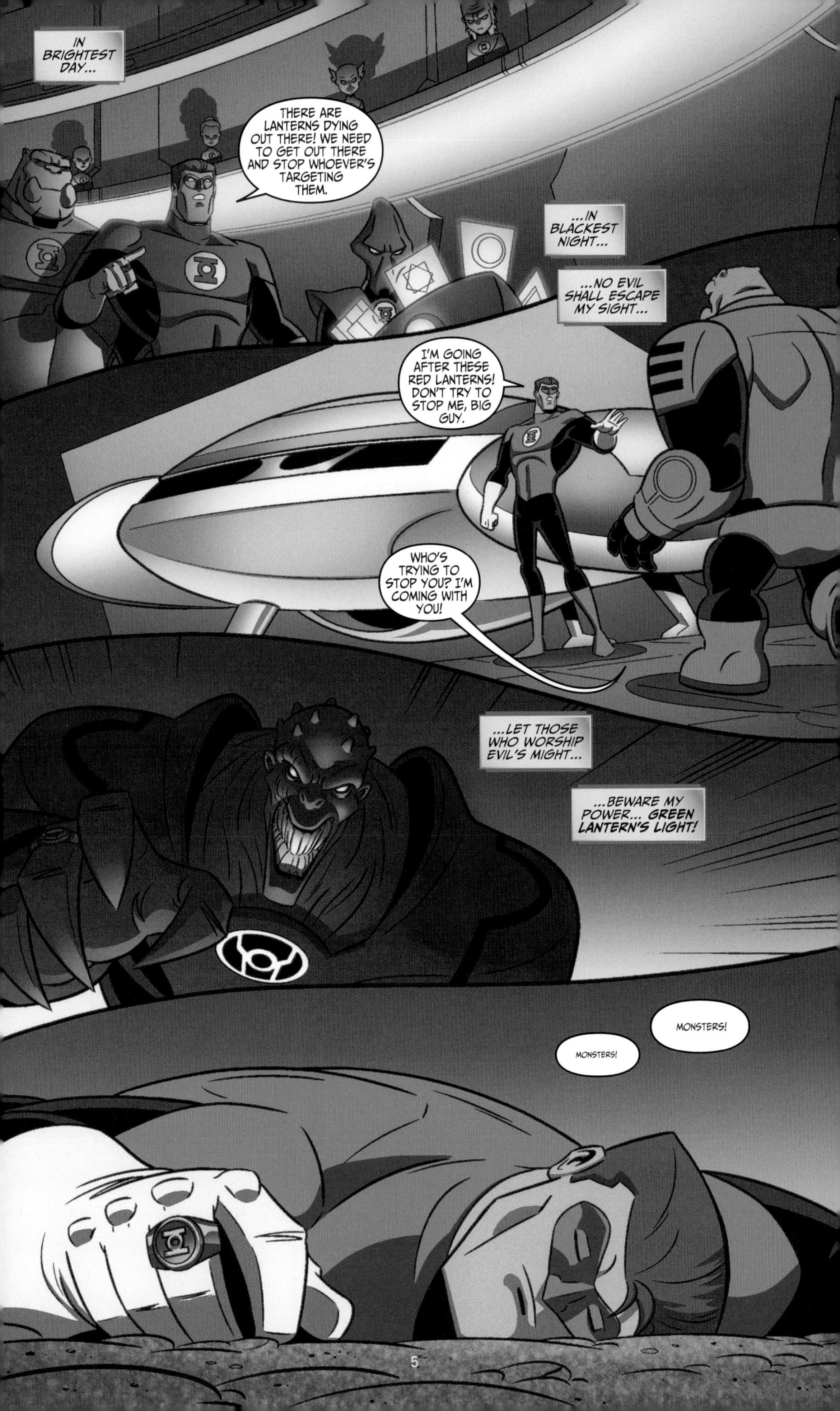
IN BRIGHTEST DAY...
THERE ARE LANTERNS DYING OUT THERE! WE NEED TO GET OUT THERE AND STOP WHOEVER'S TARGETING THEM.
...IN BLACKEST NIGHT...
...NO EVIL SHALL ESCAPE MY SIGHT...
I'M GOING AFTER THESE RED LANTERNS! DON'T TRY TO STOP ME, BIG GUY.
WHO'S TRYING TO STOP YOU? I'M COMING WITH YOU!
...LET THOSE WHO WORSHIP EVIL'S MIGHT...
...BEWARE MY POWER... GREEN LANTERN'S LIGHT!
MONSTERS!
MONSTERS!

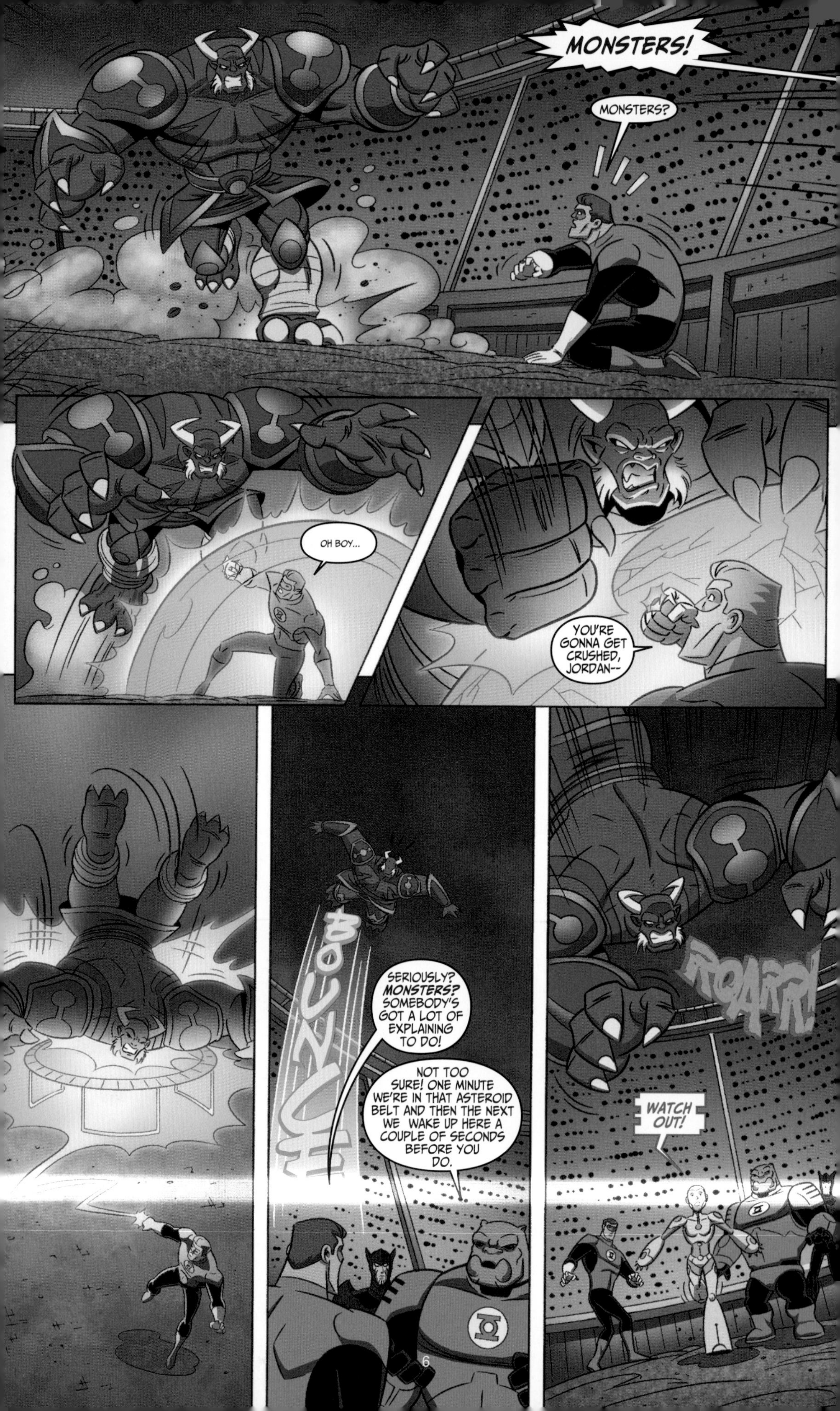

MONSTERS!
MONSTERS?
OH BOY...
YOU'RE GONNA GET CRUSHED, JORDAN--
SERIOUSLY? MONSTERS? SOMEBODY'S GOT A LOT OF EXPLAINING TO DO!
NOT TOO SURE! ONE MINUTE WE'RE IN THAT ASTEROID BELT AND THEN THE NEXT WE WAKE UP HERE A COUPLE OF SECONDS BEFORE YOU DO.
BOUNCE
ROARR!
WATCH OUT!

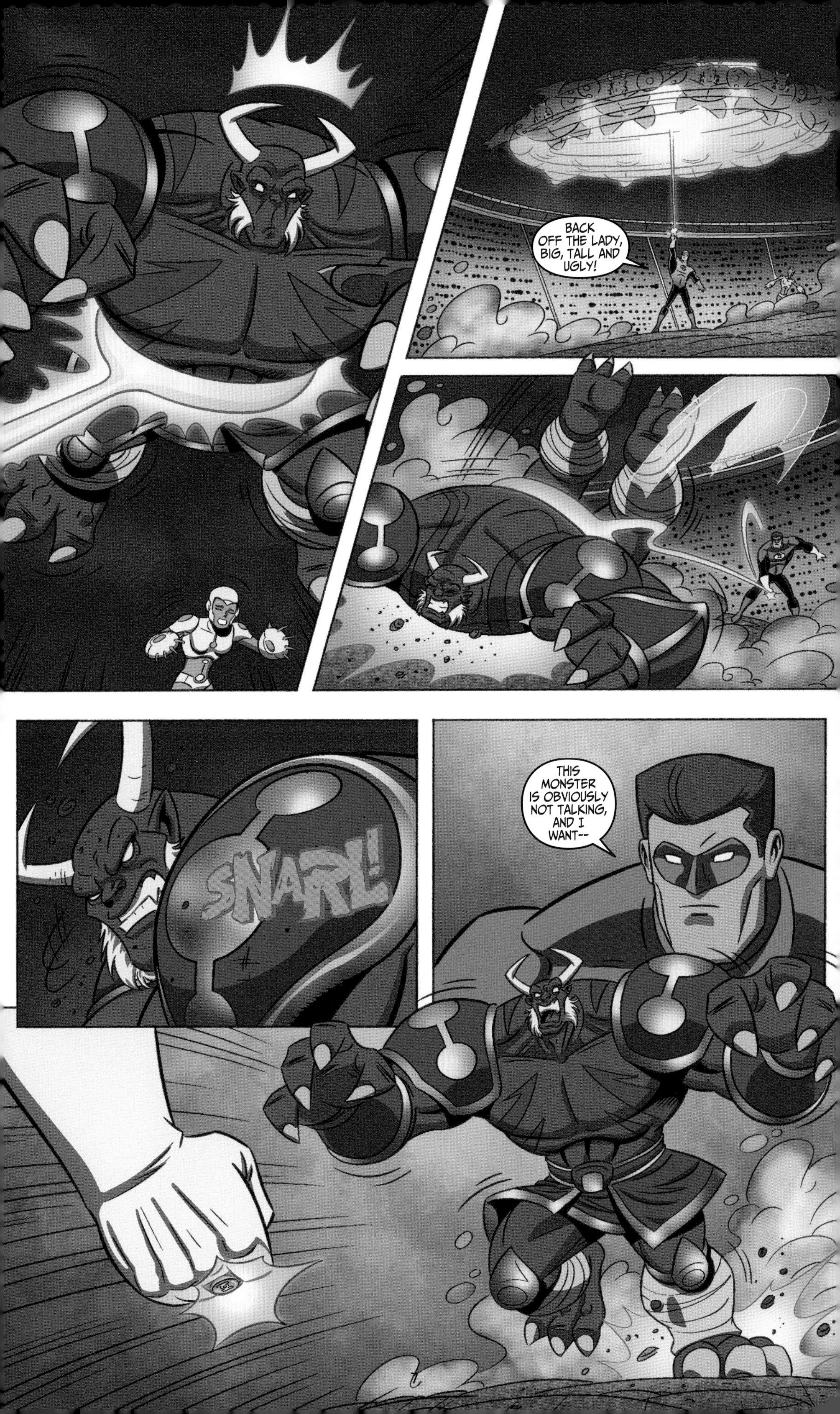
BACK OFF THE LADY, BIG, TALL AND UGLY!
SNARL!
THIS MONSTER IS OBVIOUSLY NOT TALKING, AND I WANT--

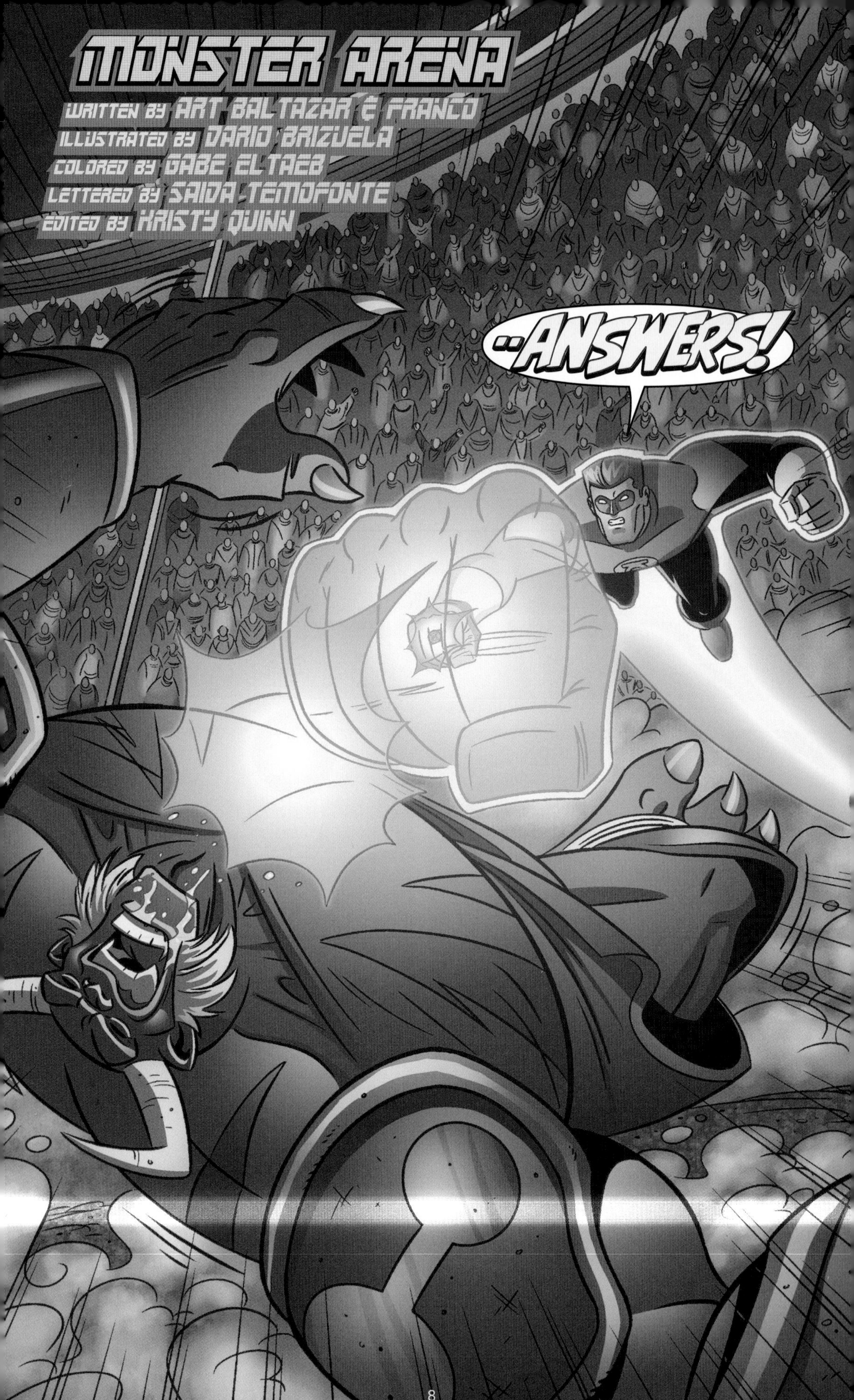
MONSTER ARENA
WRITTEN BY ART BALTAZAR & FRANCO
ILLUSTRATED BY DARIO BRIZUELA
COLORED BY GABE ELTAEB
LETTERED BY SAIDA TEMOFONTE
EDITED BY KRISTY QUINN
..ANSWERS!

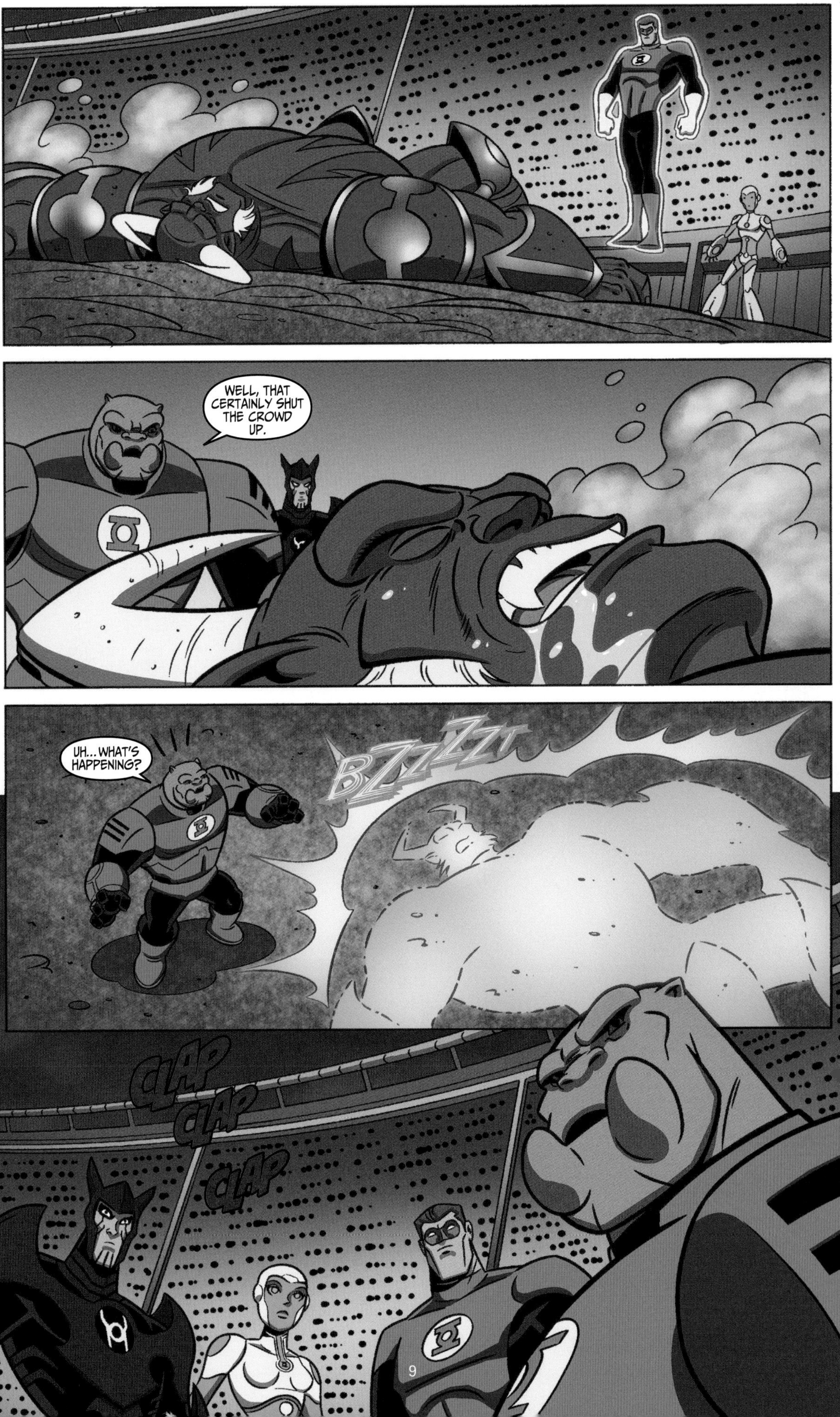
WELL, THAT CERTAINLY SHUT THE CROWD UP.
UH...WHAT'S HAPPENING?
BZZZZZT
CLAP
CLAP
CLAP

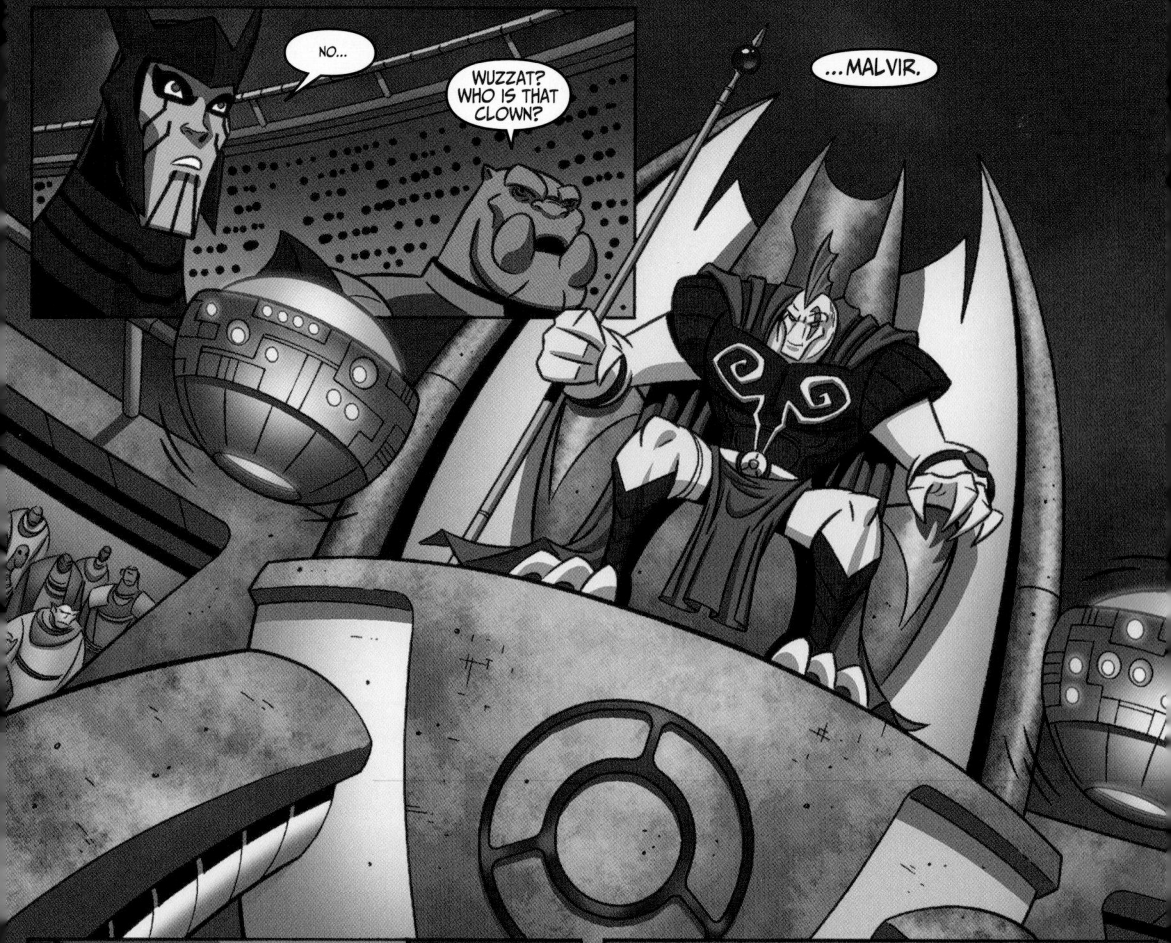
NO...
WUZZAT? WHO IS THAT CLOWN?
...MALVIR.

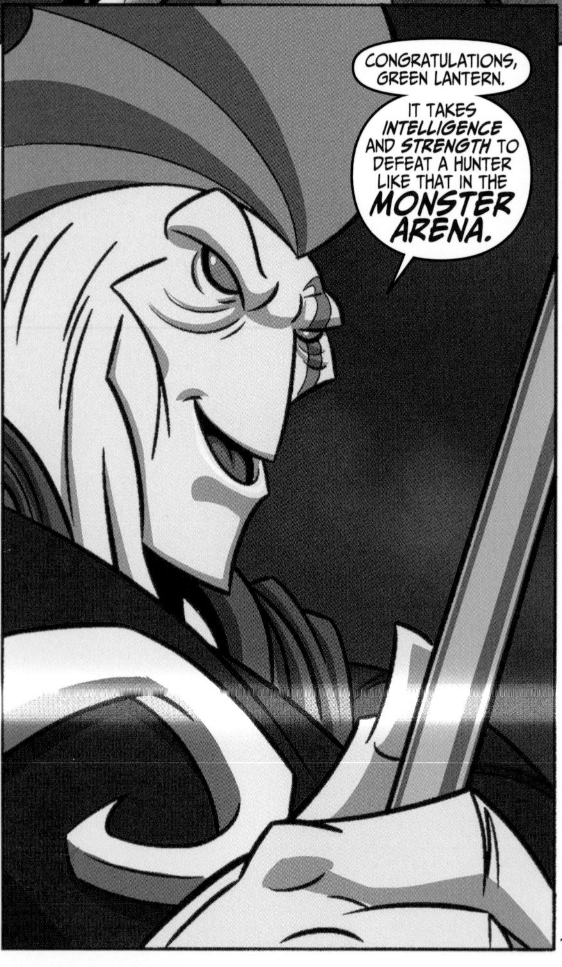
CONGRATULATIONS, GREEN LANTERN.
IT TAKES *INTELLIGENCE* AND *STRENGTH* TO DEFEAT A HUNTER LIKE THAT IN THE **MONSTER ARENA.**

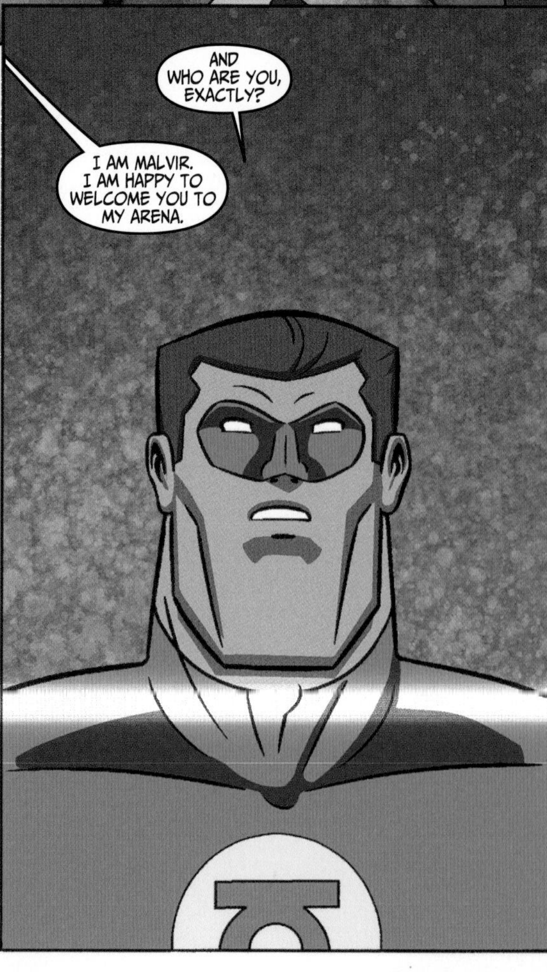
AND WHO ARE YOU, EXACTLY?
I AM MALVIR. I AM HAPPY TO WELCOME YOU TO MY ARENA.

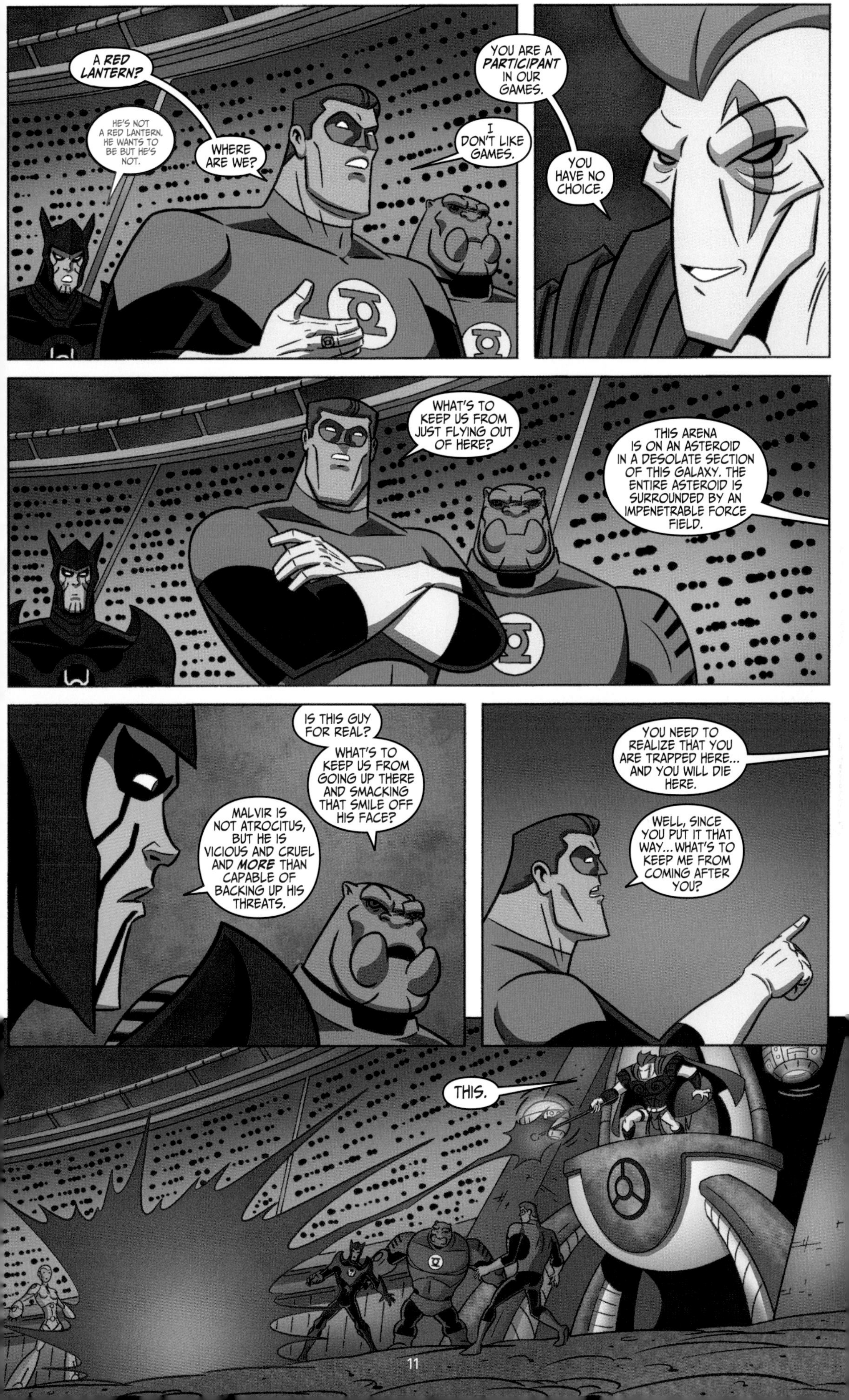

A RED LANTERN?
HE'S NOT A RED LANTERN. HE WANTS TO BE BUT HE'S NOT.
WHERE ARE WE?
I DON'T LIKE GAMES.
YOU ARE A PARTICIPANT IN OUR GAMES.
YOU HAVE NO CHOICE.
WHAT'S TO KEEP US FROM JUST FLYING OUT OF HERE?
THIS ARENA IS ON AN ASTEROID IN A DESOLATE SECTION OF THIS GALAXY. THE ENTIRE ASTEROID IS SURROUNDED BY AN IMPENETRABLE FORCE FIELD.
IS THIS GUY FOR REAL?
WHAT'S TO KEEP US FROM GOING UP THERE AND SMACKING THAT SMILE OFF HIS FACE?
MALVIR IS NOT ATROCITUS, BUT HE IS VICIOUS AND CRUEL AND MORE THAN CAPABLE OF BACKING UP HIS THREATS.
YOU NEED TO REALIZE THAT YOU ARE TRAPPED HERE... AND YOU WILL DIE HERE.
WELL, SINCE YOU PUT IT THAT WAY... WHAT'S TO KEEP ME FROM COMING AFTER YOU?
THIS.

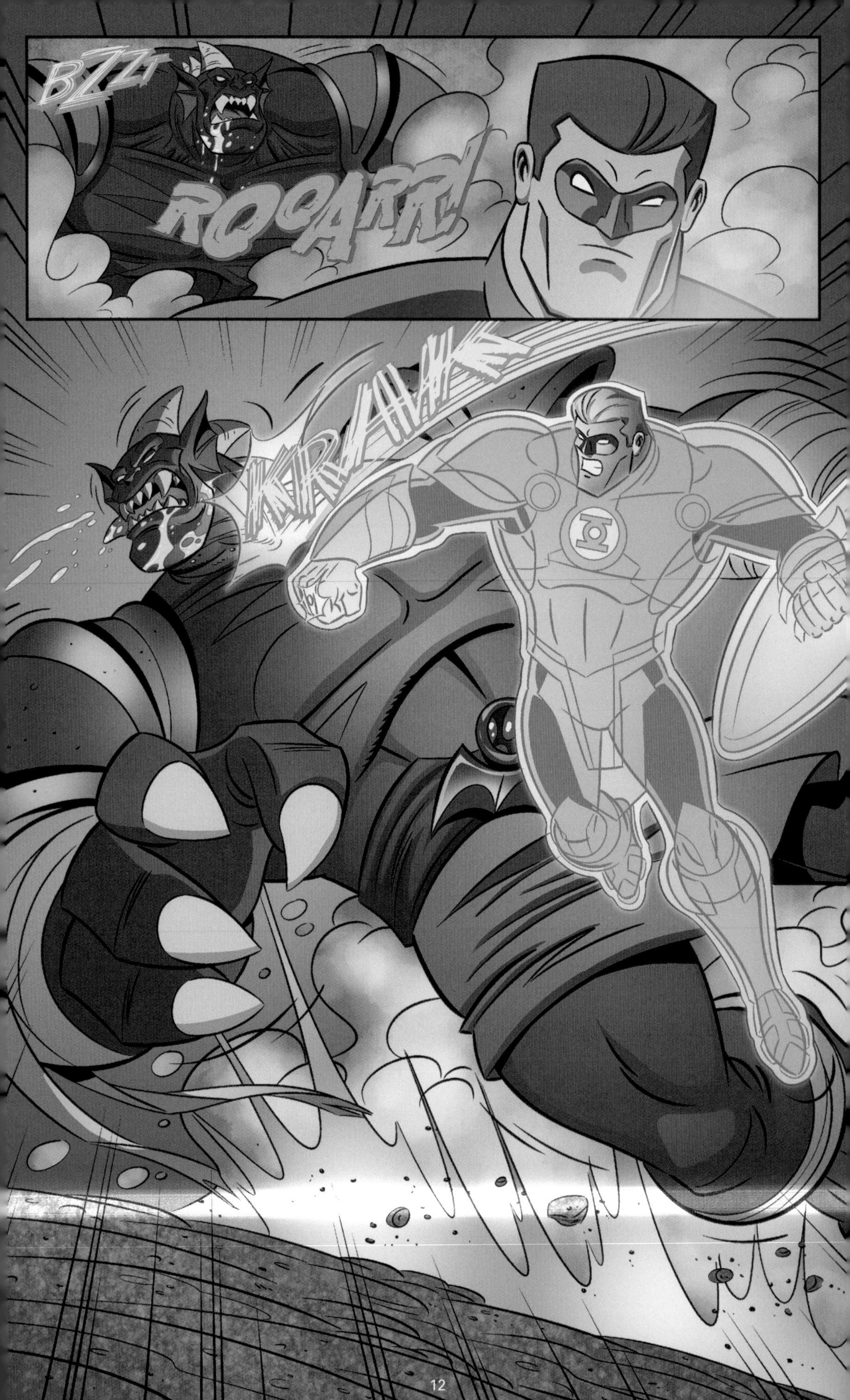
BZZT
ROOARR!
KRAAAK

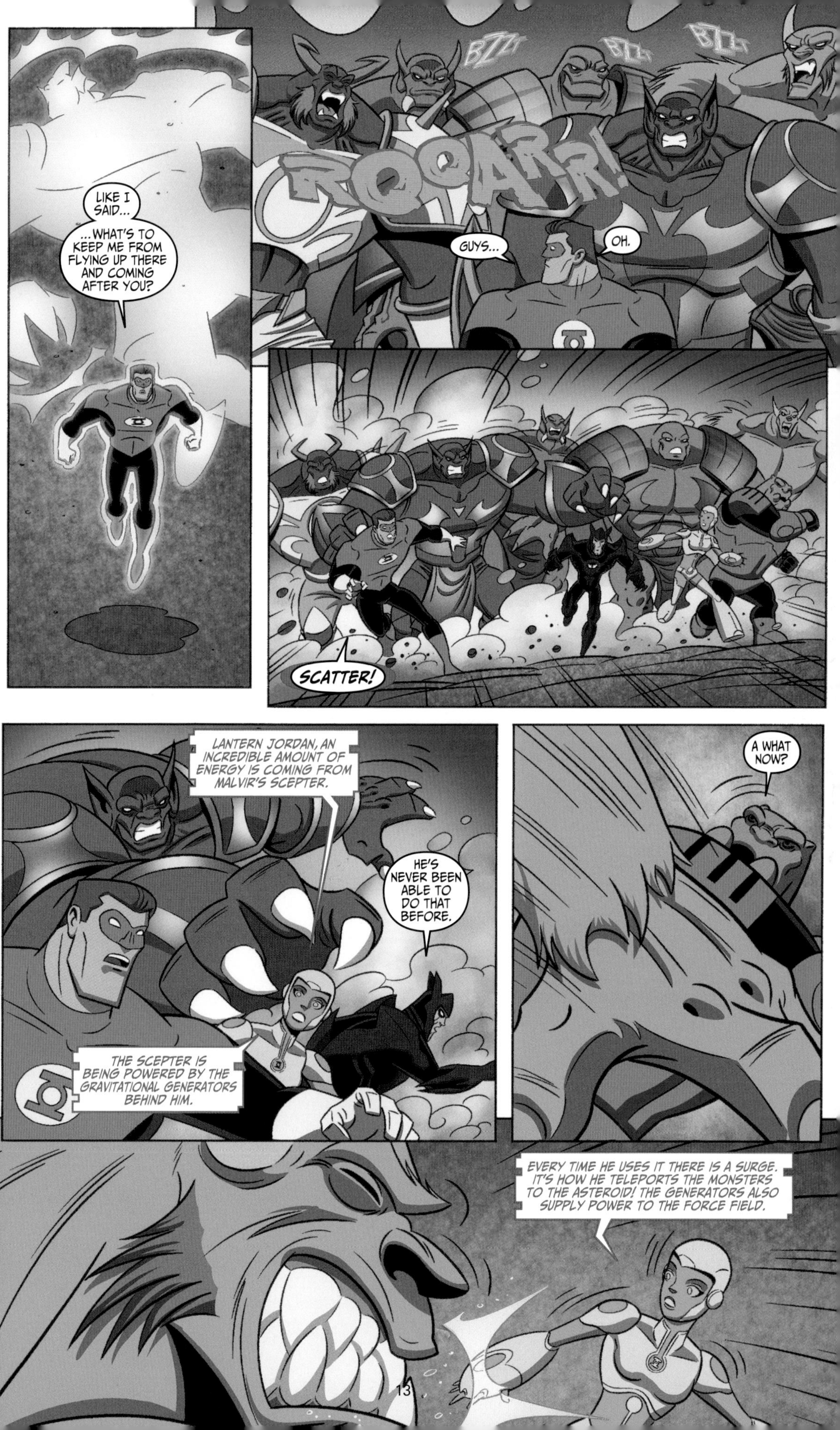
LIKE I SAID...
...WHAT'S TO KEEP ME FROM FLYING UP THERE AND COMING AFTER YOU?
BZZT
BZZT
BZZT
ROOARRR!
GUYS...
OH.
SCATTER!
LANTERN JORDAN, AN INCREDIBLE AMOUNT OF ENERGY IS COMING FROM MALVIR'S SCEPTER.
HE'S NEVER BEEN ABLE TO DO THAT BEFORE.
THE SCEPTER IS BEING POWERED BY THE GRAVITATIONAL GENERATORS BEHIND HIM.
A WHAT NOW?
EVERY TIME HE USES IT THERE IS A SURGE. IT'S HOW HE TELEPORTS THE MONSTERS TO THE ASTEROID! THE GENERATORS ALSO SUPPLY POWER TO THE FORCE FIELD.

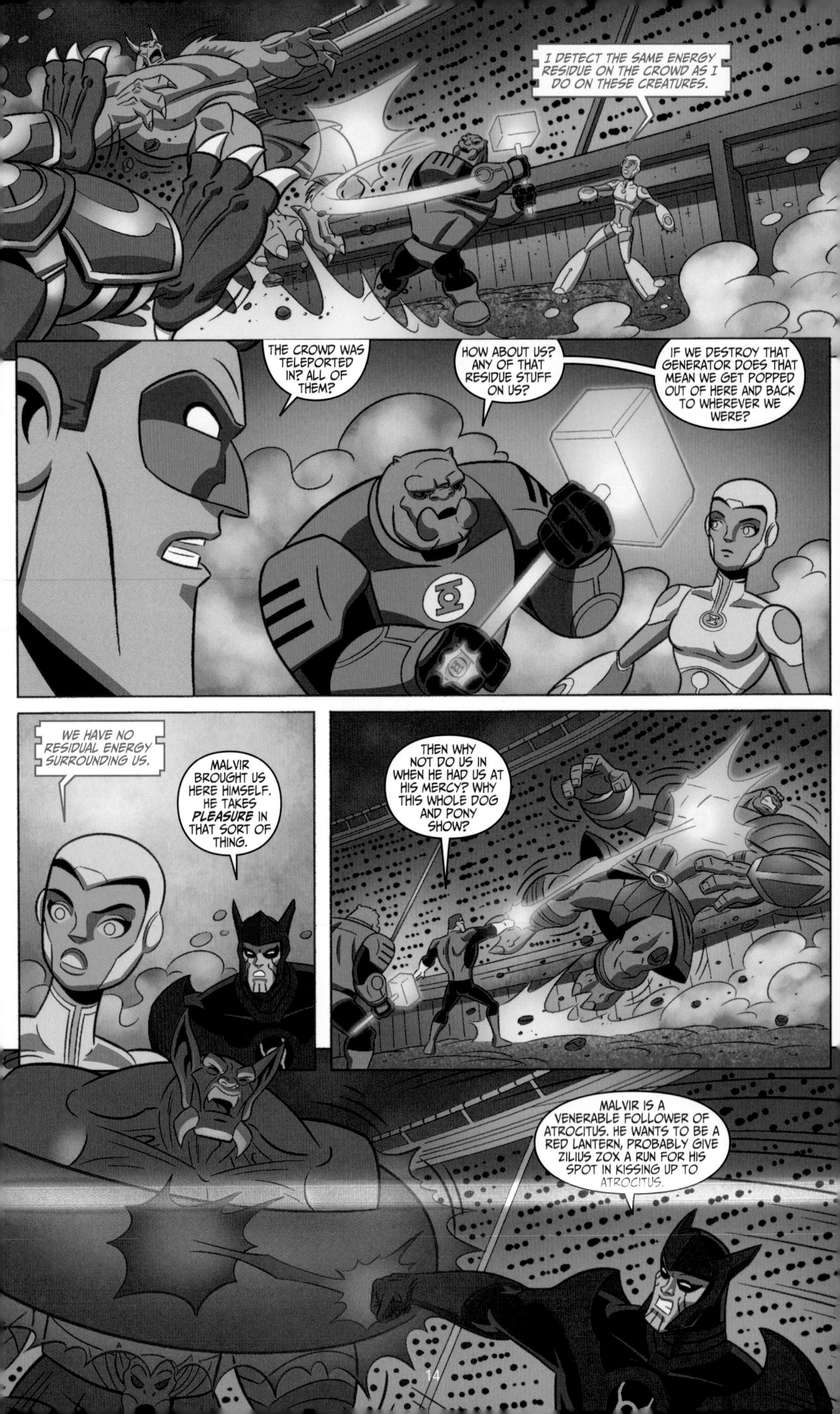
I DETECT THE SAME ENERGY RESIDUE ON THE CROWD AS I DO ON THESE CREATURES.
THE CROWD WAS TELEPORTED IN? ALL OF THEM?
HOW ABOUT US? ANY OF THAT RESIDUE STUFF ON US?
IF WE DESTROY THAT GENERATOR DOES THAT MEAN WE GET POPPED OUT OF HERE AND BACK TO WHEREVER WE WERE?
WE HAVE NO RESIDUAL ENERGY SURROUNDING US.
MALVIR BROUGHT US HERE HIMSELF. HE TAKES ***PLEASURE*** IN THAT SORT OF THING.
THEN WHY NOT DO US IN WHEN HE HAD US AT HIS MERCY? WHY THIS WHOLE DOG AND PONY SHOW?
MALVIR IS A VENERABLE FOLLOWER OF ATROCITUS. HE WANTS TO BE A RED LANTERN, PROBABLY GIVE ZILIUS ZOX A RUN FOR HIS SPOT IN KISSING UP TO ATROCITUS.

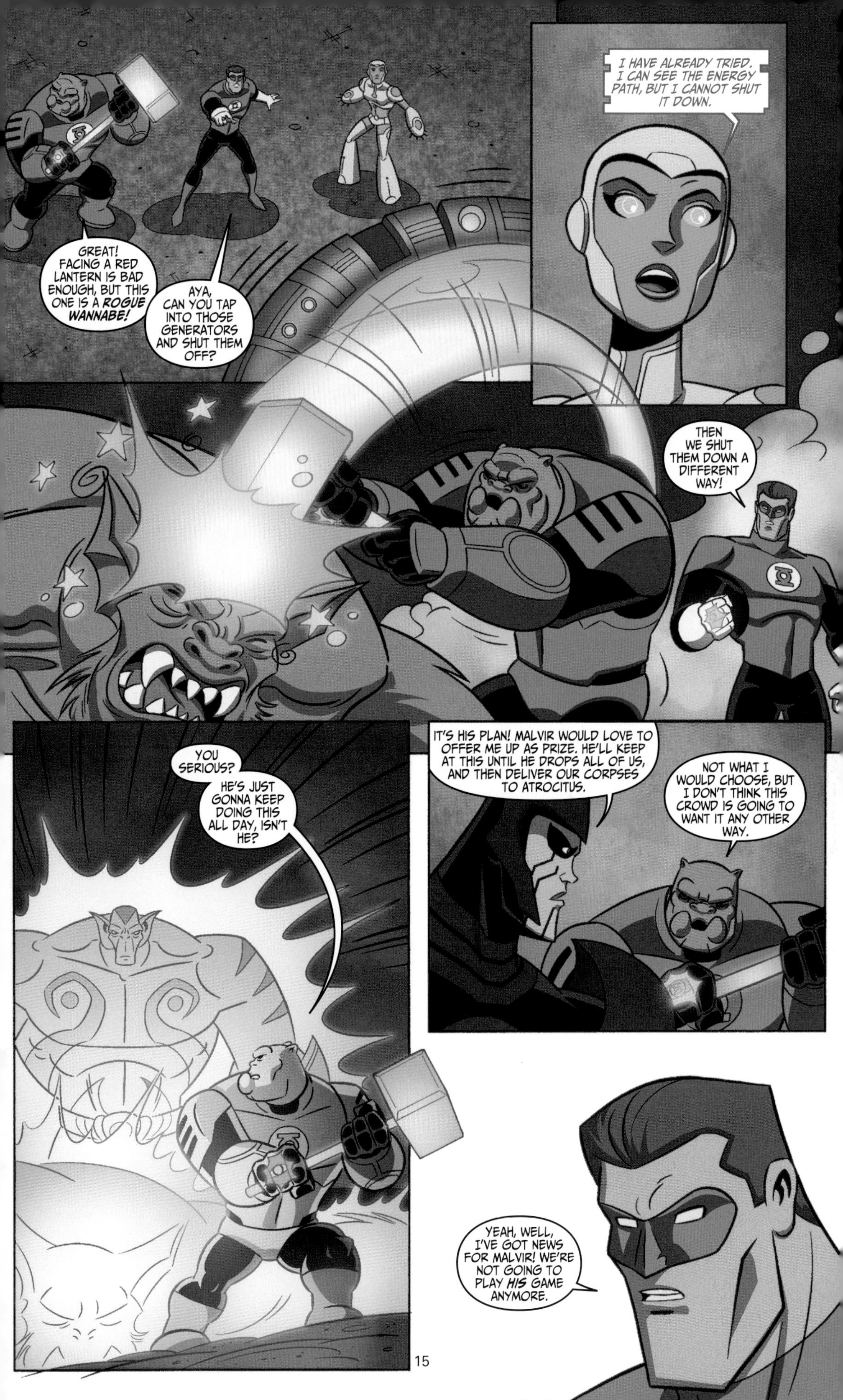
GREAT! FACING A RED LANTERN IS BAD ENOUGH, BUT THIS ONE IS A ROGUE WANNABE!
AYA, CAN YOU TAP INTO THOSE GENERATORS AND SHUT THEM OFF?
I HAVE ALREADY TRIED. I CAN SEE THE ENERGY PATH, BUT I CANNOT SHUT IT DOWN.
THEN WE SHUT THEM DOWN A DIFFERENT WAY!
YOU SERIOUS?
HE'S JUST GONNA KEEP DOING THIS ALL DAY, ISN'T HE?
IT'S HIS PLAN! MALVIR WOULD LOVE TO OFFER ME UP AS PRIZE. HE'LL KEEP AT THIS UNTIL HE DROPS ALL OF US, AND THEN DELIVER OUR CORPSES TO ATROCITUS.
NOT WHAT I WOULD CHOOSE, BUT I DON'T THINK THIS CROWD IS GOING TO WANT IT ANY OTHER WAY.
YEAH, WELL, I'VE GOT NEWS FOR MALVIR! WE'RE NOT GOING TO PLAY HIS GAME ANYMORE.

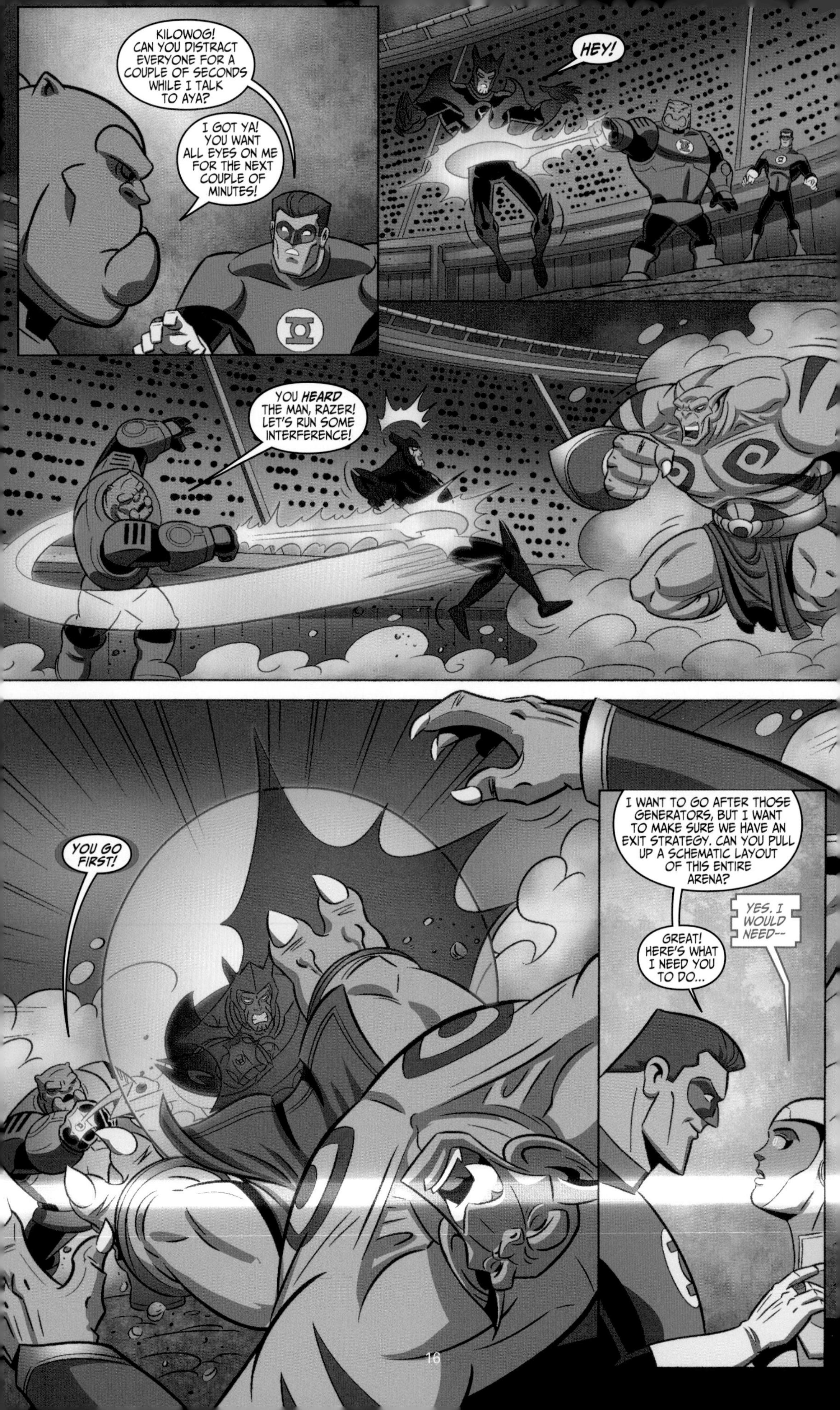
KILOWOG! CAN YOU DISTRACT EVERYONE FOR A COUPLE OF SECONDS WHILE I TALK TO AYA?
I GOT YA! YOU WANT ALL EYES ON ME FOR THE NEXT COUPLE OF MINUTES!
HEY!
YOU HEARD THE MAN, RAZER! LET'S RUN SOME INTERFERENCE!
YOU GO FIRST!
I WANT TO GO AFTER THOSE GENERATORS, BUT I WANT TO MAKE SURE WE HAVE AN EXIT STRATEGY. CAN YOU PULL UP A SCHEMATIC LAYOUT OF THIS ENTIRE ARENA?
YES. I WOULD NEED--
GREAT! HERE'S WHAT I NEED YOU TO DO...

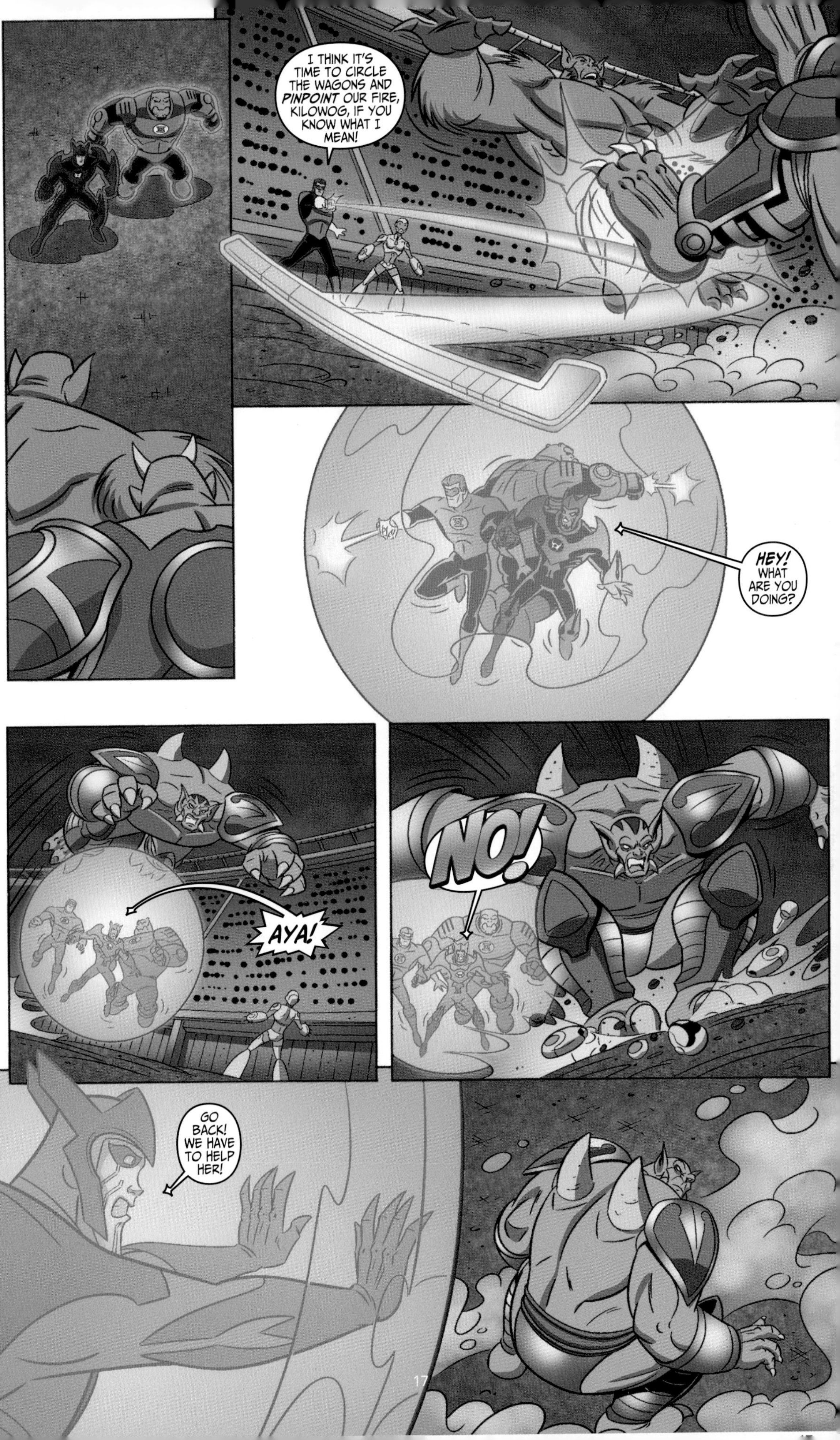
I THINK IT'S TIME TO CIRCLE THE WAGONS AND PINPOINT OUR FIRE, KILOWOG, IF YOU KNOW WHAT I MEAN!
HEY! WHAT ARE YOU DOING?
AYA!
NO!
GO BACK! WE HAVE TO HELP HER!

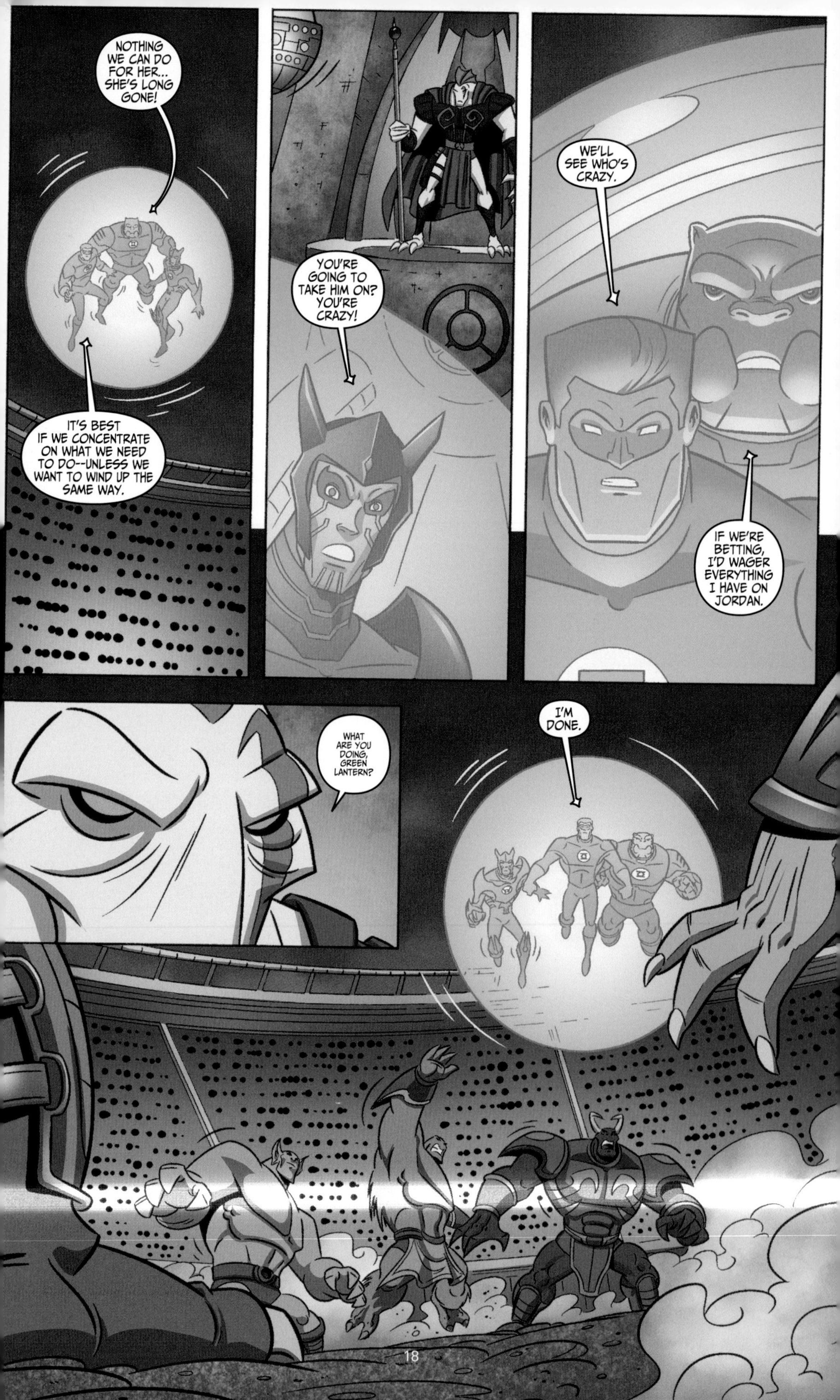
NOTHING WE CAN DO FOR HER... SHE'S LONG GONE!
IT'S BEST IF WE CONCENTRATE ON WHAT WE NEED TO DO--UNLESS WE WANT TO WIND UP THE SAME WAY.
YOU'RE GOING TO TAKE HIM ON? YOU'RE CRAZY!
WE'LL SEE WHO'S CRAZY.
IF WE'RE BETTING, I'D WAGER EVERYTHING I HAVE ON JORDAN.
WHAT ARE YOU DOING, GREEN LANTERN?
I'M DONE.

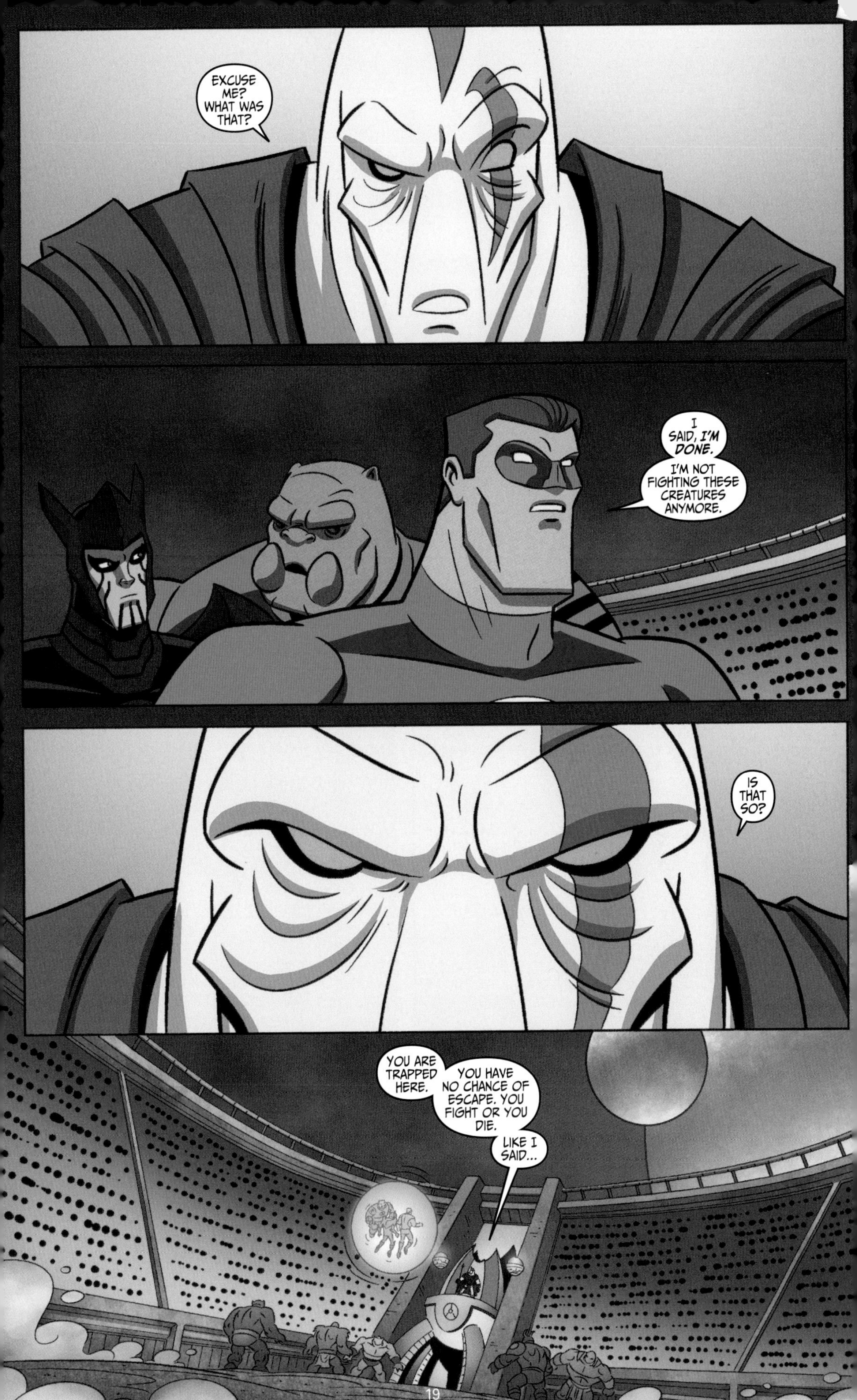
EXCUSE ME? WHAT WAS THAT?
I SAID, *I'M DONE.*
I'M NOT FIGHTING THESE CREATURES ANYMORE.
IS THAT SO?
YOU ARE TRAPPED HERE.
YOU HAVE NO CHANCE OF ESCAPE. YOU FIGHT OR YOU DIE.
LIKE I SAID...

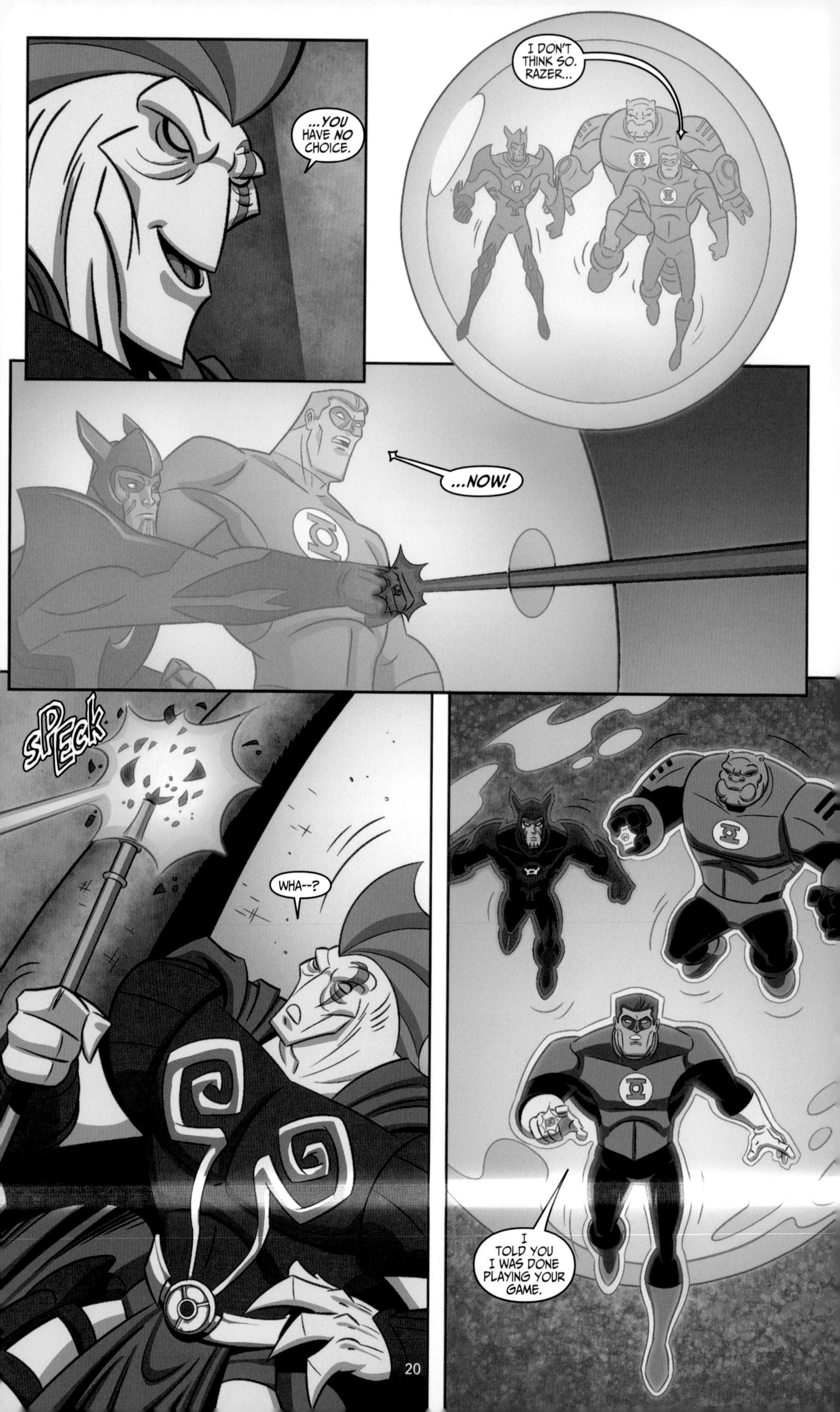

...YOU HAVE NO CHOICE.
I DON'T THINK SO, RAZER...
...NOW!
SPECK
WHA--?
I TOLD YOU I WAS DONE PLAYING YOUR GAME.

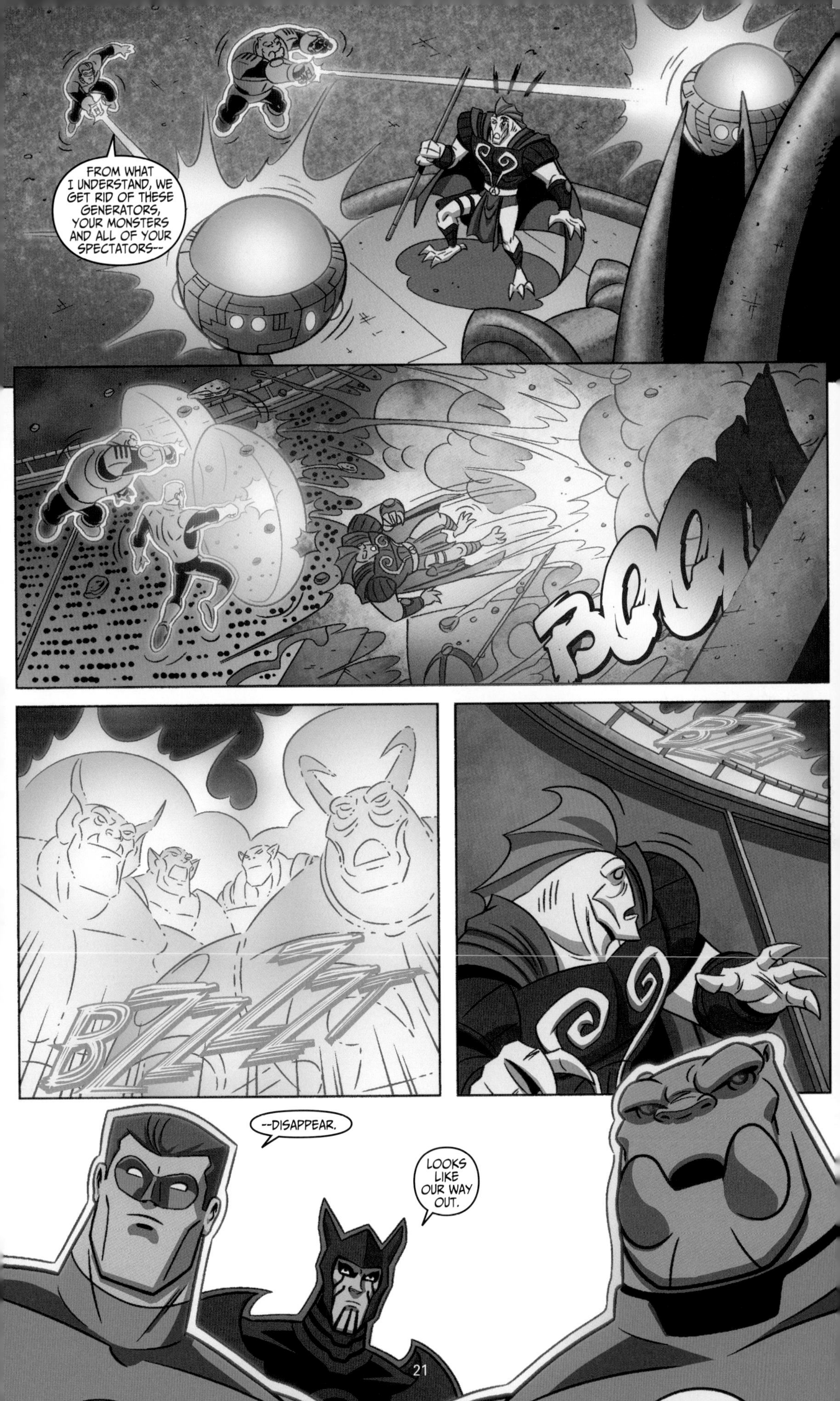

FROM WHAT I UNDERSTAND, WE GET RID OF THESE GENERATORS, YOUR MONSTERS AND ALL OF YOUR SPECTATORS--
BOOM
BZZZT
BZZT
--DISAPPEAR.
LOOKS LIKE OUR WAY OUT.

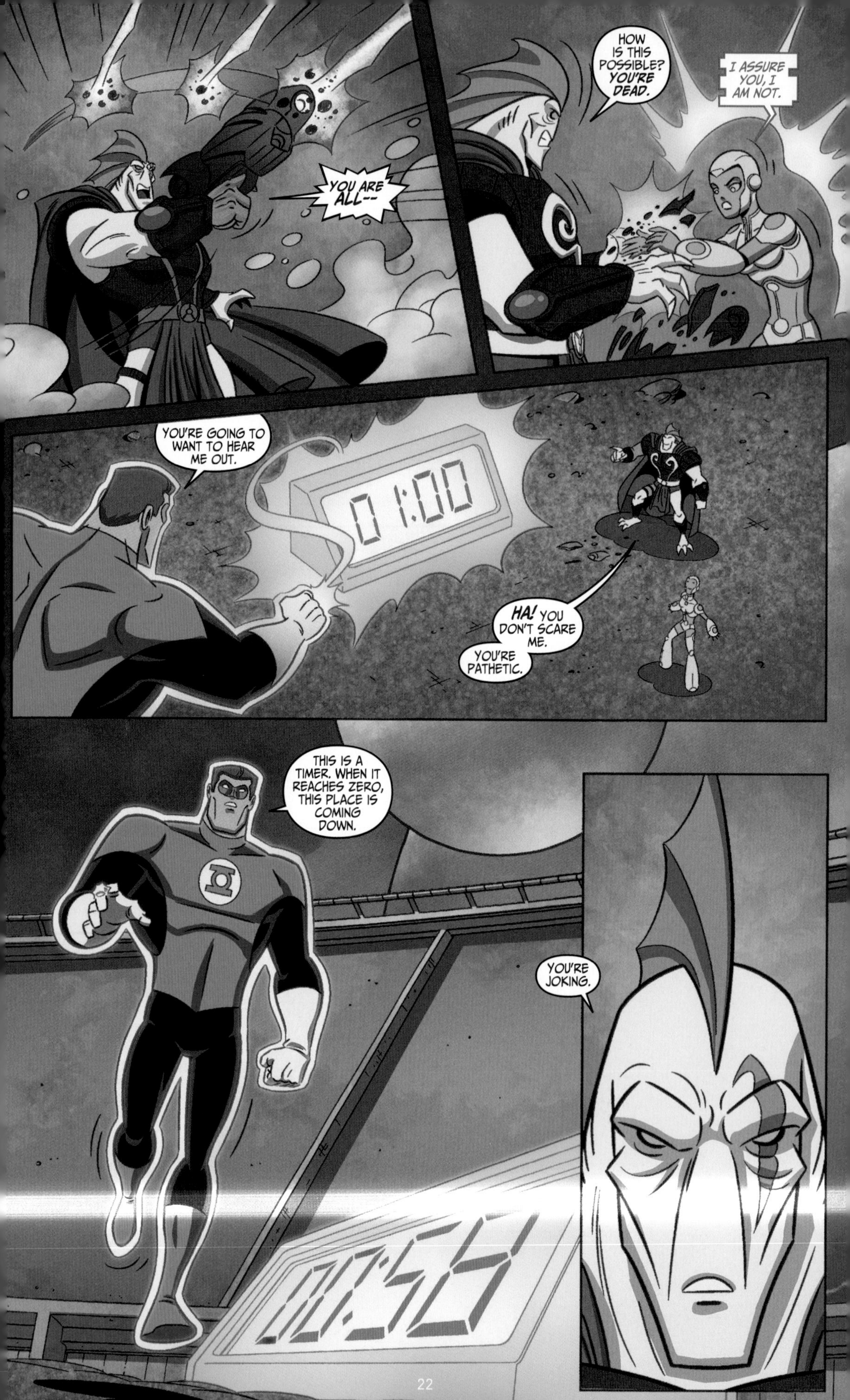
YOU ARE ALL--
HOW IS THIS POSSIBLE? YOU'RE DEAD.
I ASSURE YOU, I AM NOT.
YOU'RE GOING TO WANT TO HEAR ME OUT.
01:00
HA! YOU DON'T SCARE ME.
YOU'RE PATHETIC.
THIS IS A TIMER. WHEN IT REACHES ZERO, THIS PLACE IS COMING DOWN.
YOU'RE JOKING.

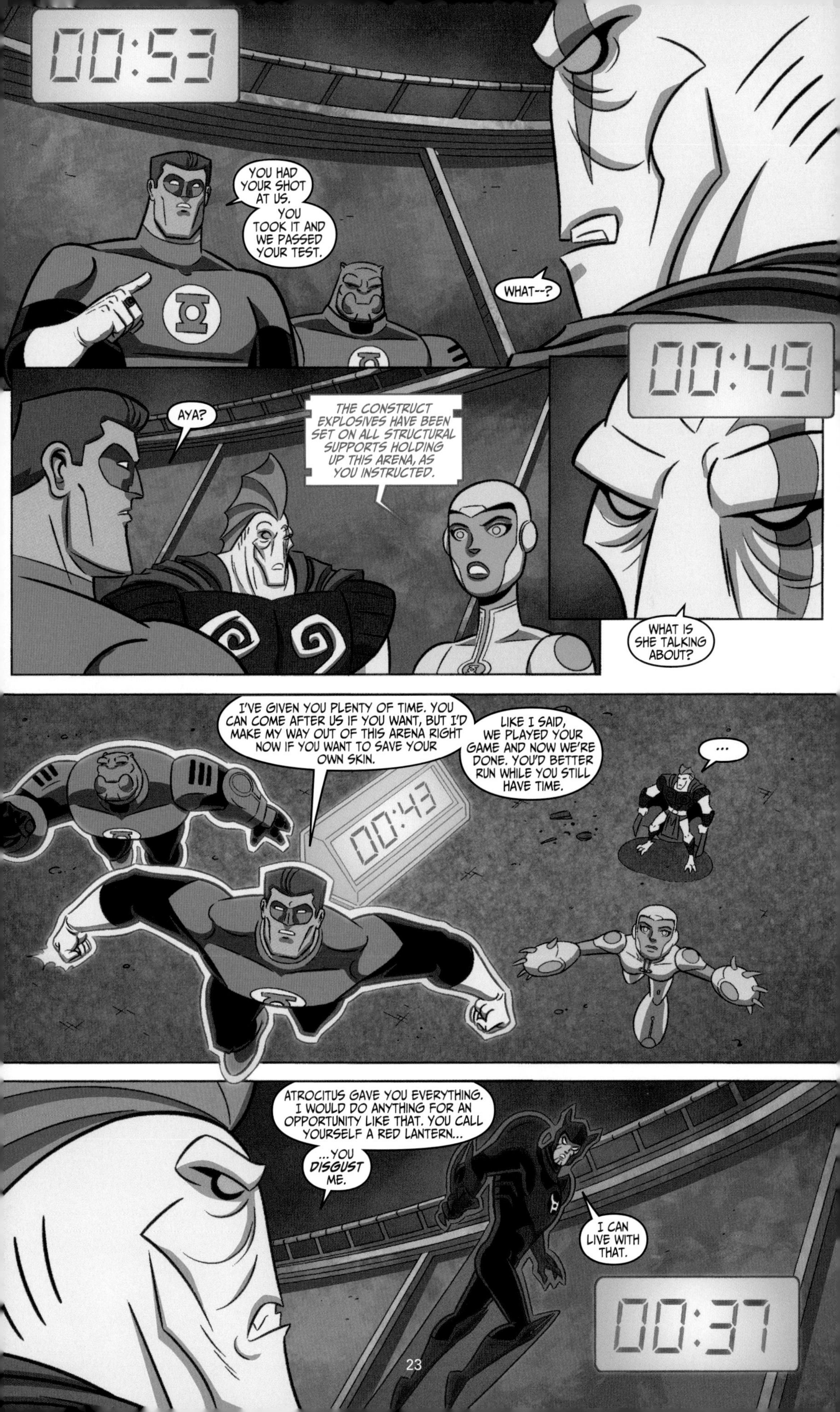
00:53
YOU HAD YOUR SHOT AT US.
YOU TOOK IT AND WE PASSED YOUR TEST.
WHAT--?
00:49
AYA?
THE CONSTRUCT EXPLOSIVES HAVE BEEN SET ON ALL STRUCTURAL SUPPORTS HOLDING UP THIS ARENA, AS YOU INSTRUCTED.
WHAT IS SHE TALKING ABOUT?
I'VE GIVEN YOU PLENTY OF TIME. YOU CAN COME AFTER US IF YOU WANT, BUT I'D MAKE MY WAY OUT OF THIS ARENA RIGHT NOW IF YOU WANT TO SAVE YOUR OWN SKIN.
LIKE I SAID, WE PLAYED YOUR GAME AND NOW WE'RE DONE. YOU'D BETTER RUN WHILE YOU STILL HAVE TIME.
00:43
...
ATROCITUS GAVE YOU EVERYTHING. I WOULD DO ANYTHING FOR AN OPPORTUNITY LIKE THAT. YOU CALL YOURSELF A RED LANTERN...
...YOU DISGUST ME.
I CAN LIVE WITH THAT.
00:37

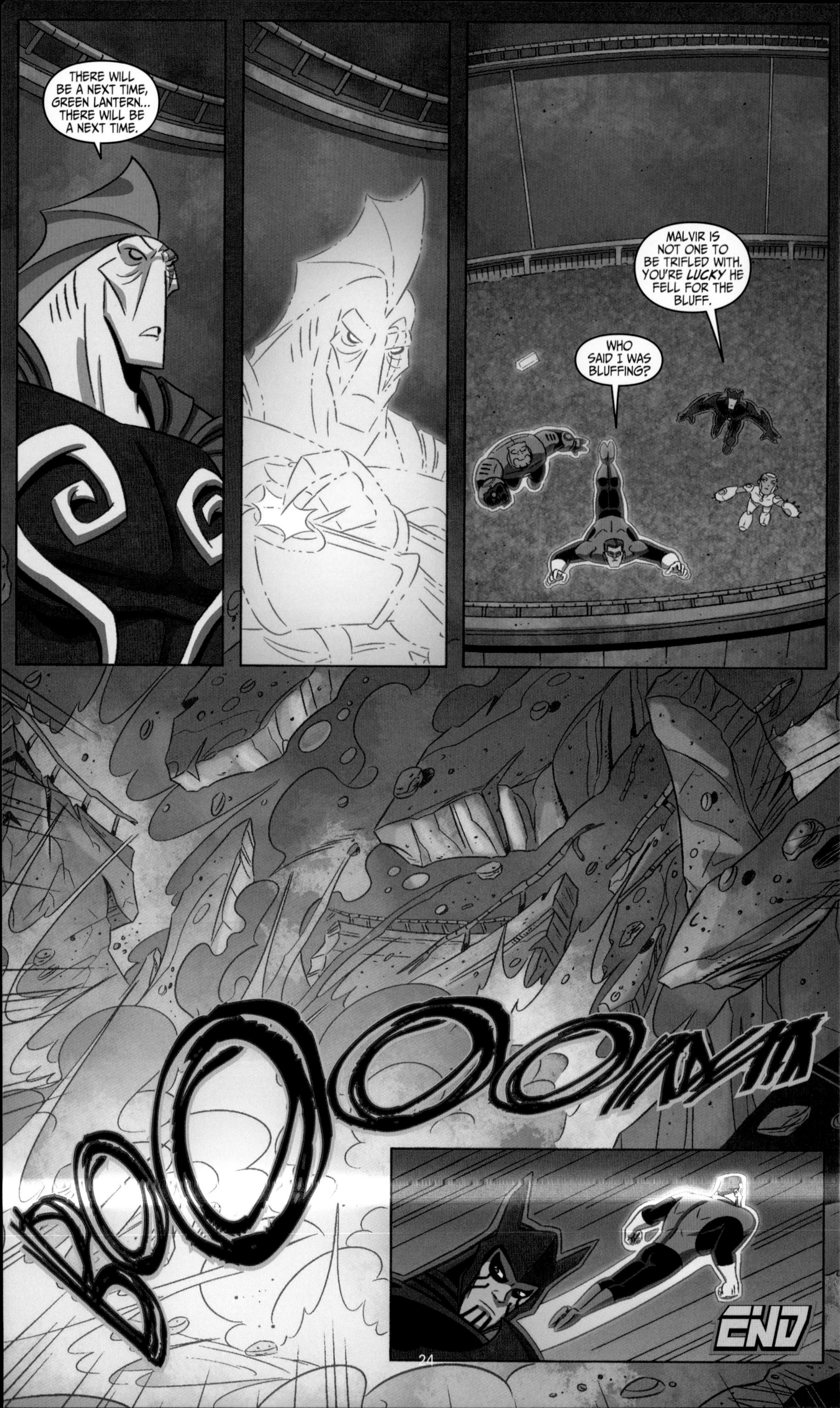

THERE WILL BE A NEXT TIME, GREEN LANTERN... THERE WILL BE A NEXT TIME.
MALVIR IS NOT ONE TO BE TRIFLED WITH. YOU'RE LUCKY HE FELL FOR THE BLUFF.
WHO SAID I WAS BLUFFING?
BOOOOOM!!
END

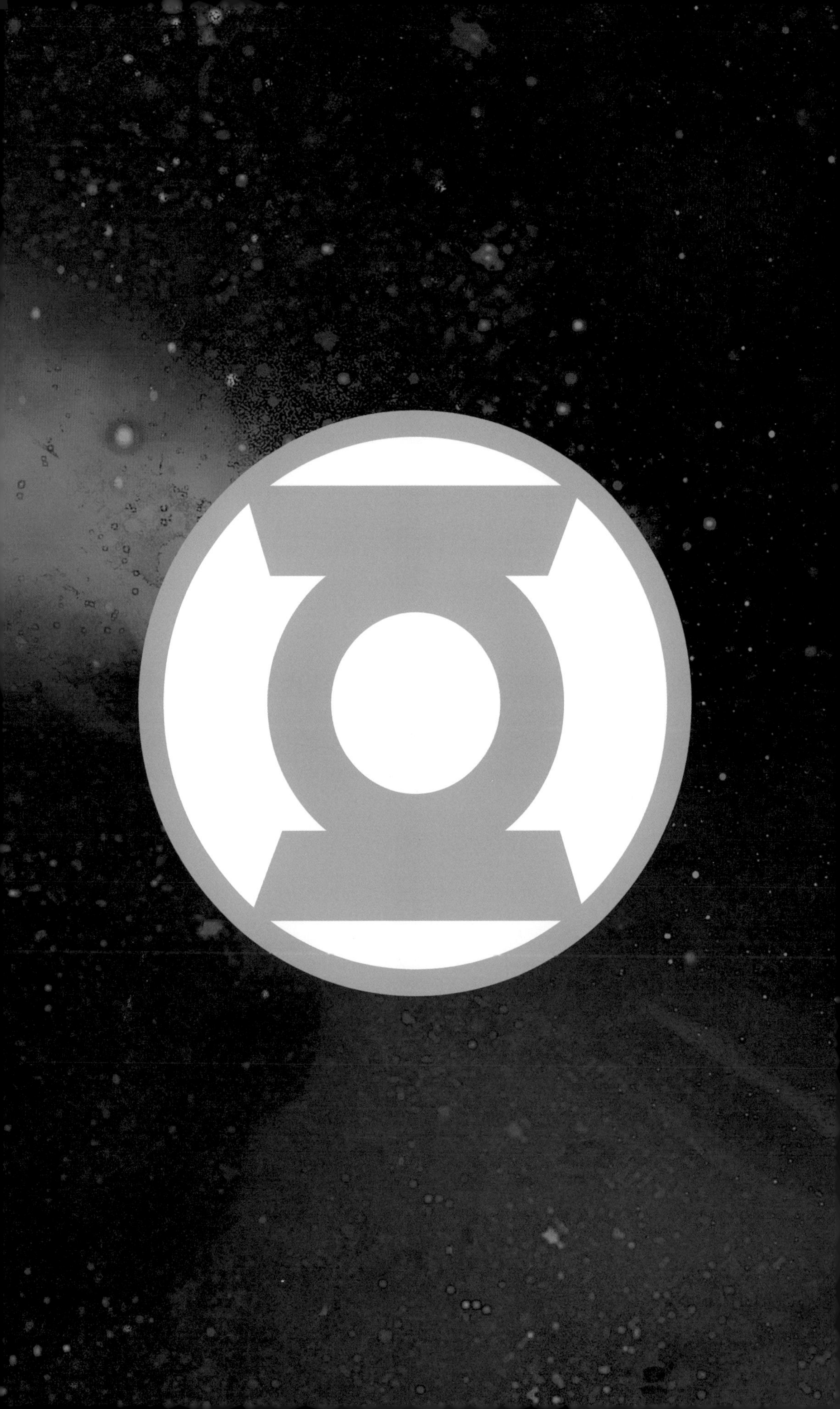

DRAW YOUR OWN GREEN LANTERN
KILOWOG!

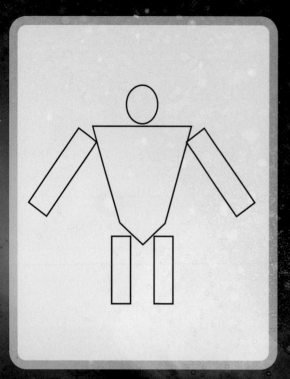

1.) Using a pencil, start with some basic shapes to build a "body."

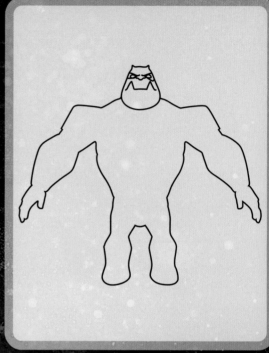

2.) Smooth your outline, and begin adding facial features.

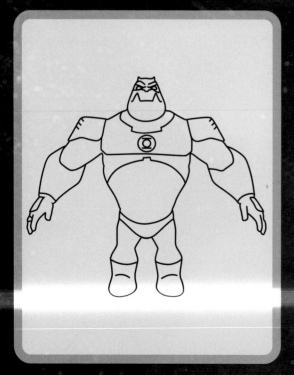

3.) Add in costume details, like Kilowog's suit, gloves, and Green Lantern symbol.

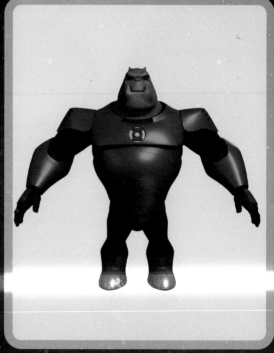

4.) Fill in the colors with crayons or markers.

CREATORS

ART BALTAZAR *writer*

Art Baltazar is a cartoonist machine from the heart of Chicago! He defines cartoons and comics not only as an art style, but as a way of life. Currently, Art is the creative force behind *The New York Times* best-selling, Eisner Award-winning, DC Comics series Tiny Titans, and the co-writer for *Billy Batson and the Magic of SHAZAM!* and co-creator of the Superman Family Adventures series. Art is living the dream! He draws comics and never has to leave the house. He lives with his lovely wife, Rose, big boy Sonny, little boy Gordon, and little girl Audrey. Right on!

FRANCO AURELIANI *writer*

Bronx, New York-born writer and artist Franco Aureliani has been drawing comics since he could hold a crayon. Currently residing in upstate New York with his wife, Ivette, and son, Nicolas, Franco spends most of his days in a Batcave-like studio where he produces DC's Tiny Titans comics. In 1995, Franco founded Blindwolf Studios, an independent art studio where he and fellow creators can create children's comics. Franco is the creator, artist, and writer of *Weirdsville*, *L'il Creeps*, and *Eagle All Star*, as well as the co-creator and writer of *Patrick the Wolf Boy*. When he's not writing and drawing, Franco also teaches high school art.

DARIO BRIZUELA *illustrator*

Dario Brizuela is a professional comic book artist. He's illustrated some of today's most popular characters, including Batman, Green Lantern, Teenage Mutant Ninja Turtles, Thor, Iron Man, and Transformers. His best-known works for DC Comics include the series DC Super Friends, Justice League Unlimited, and Batman: The Brave and the Bold.

GLOSSARY

asteroid (ASS-tuh-roid) — a very small planet that travels around the sun

bluff (BLUHF) — pretend to be in a stronger position than you really are

desolate (DESS-uh-luht) — deserted, or sad and lonely

galaxy (GAL-uhk-see) — a very large group of stars and planets

impenetrable (im-PEN-i-truh-buhl) — cannot be entered or pierced

mercy (MUR-see) — if you show mercy to someone, you do not treat or punish the person as severely as he or she may deserve

scepter (SEP-tur) —a rod or staff that is usually carried as a symbol of authority

wager (WAY-jur) — a bet

VISUAL QUESTIONS

1. Razer, Kilowog, Aya, and Hal make a good team. Identify a few panels in this book where they worked together to defeat a foe.

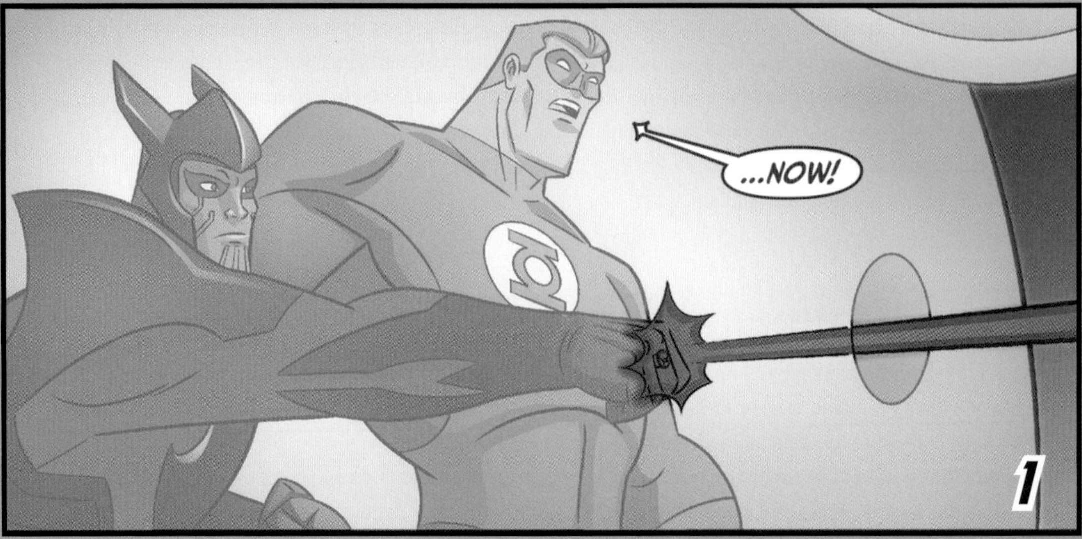
...NOW!
1

2. Razer's dialogue balloon in the panel below has a smaller text size and a red circle around it. Why?

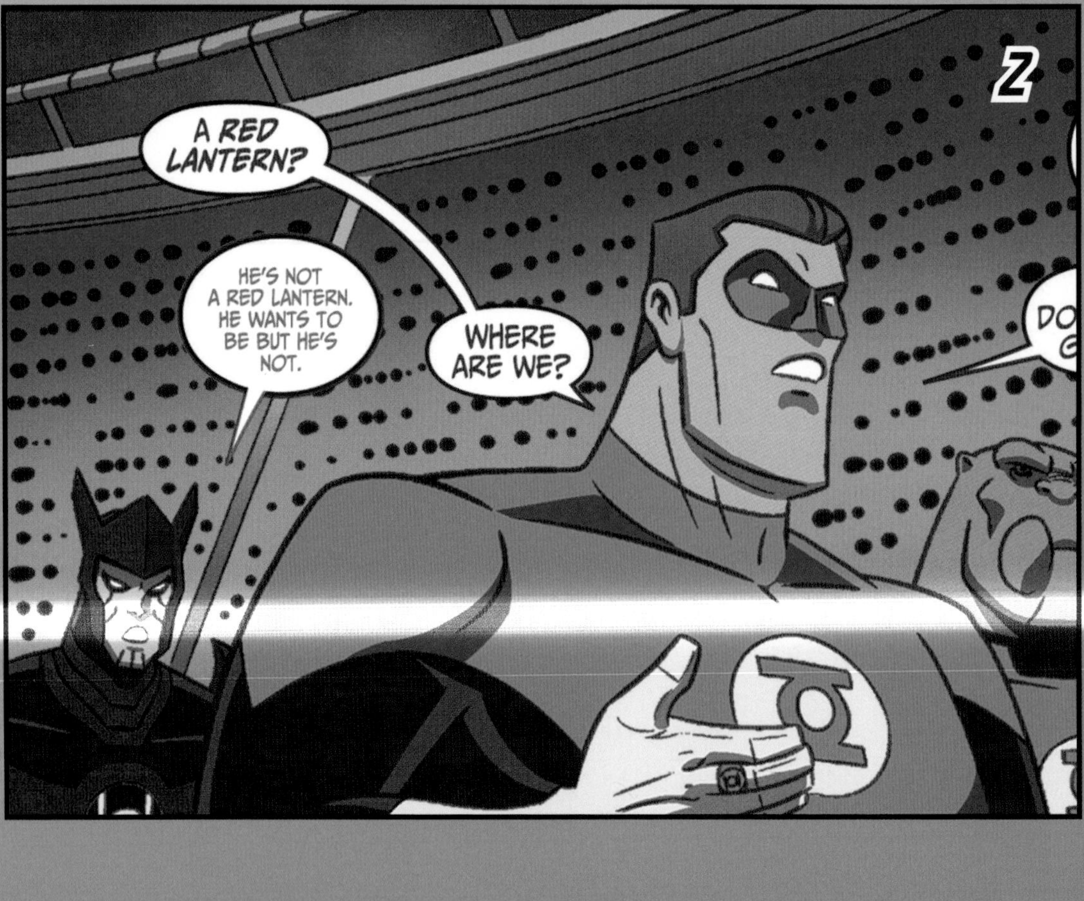
2
A RED LANTERN?
HE'S NOT A RED LANTERN. HE WANTS TO BE BUT HE'S NOT.
WHERE ARE WE?

3. Why do you think Hal decided to let Malvir go? What would you have done with the wannabe Red Lantern?

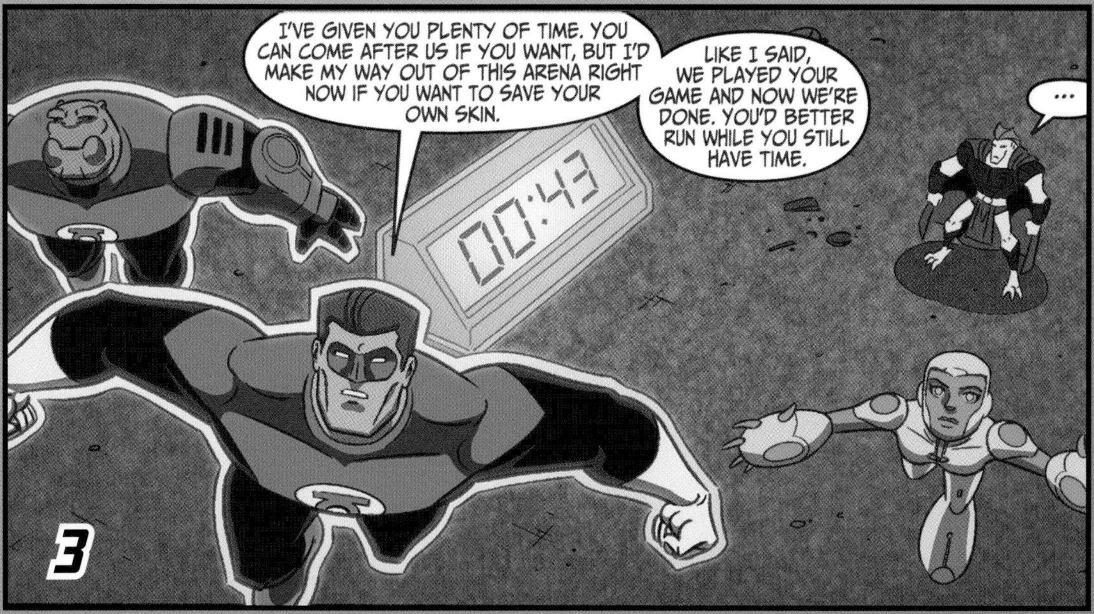
I'VE GIVEN YOU PLENTY OF TIME. YOU CAN COME AFTER US IF YOU WANT, BUT I'D MAKE MY WAY OUT OF THIS ARENA RIGHT NOW IF YOU WANT TO SAVE YOUR OWN SKIN.
LIKE I SAID, WE PLAYED YOUR GAME AND NOW WE'RE DONE. YOU'D BETTER RUN WHILE YOU STILL HAVE TIME.
...
00:43
3

4. Hal is able to use his power ring to protect himself in battle. In this panel, he creates a force field around his body and a shield for his hand. What other ways could Hal use his ring to defend himself?

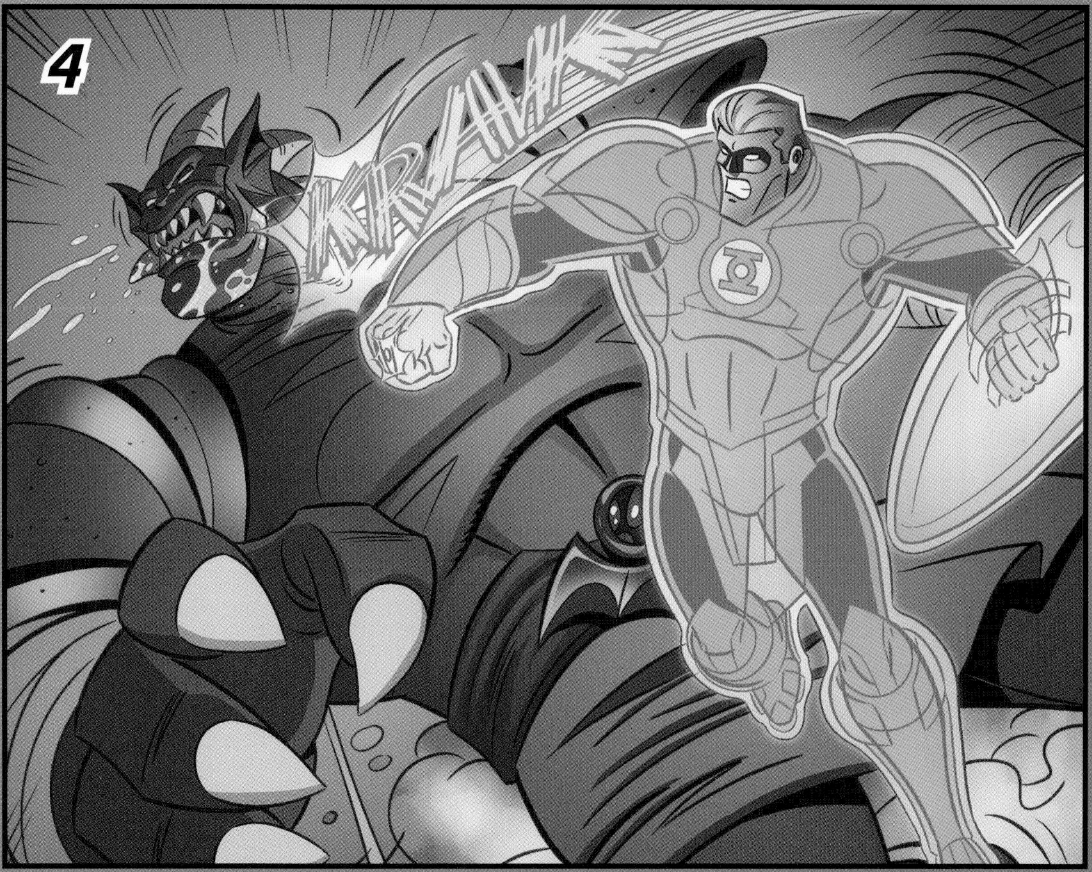
4

READ THEM ALL!

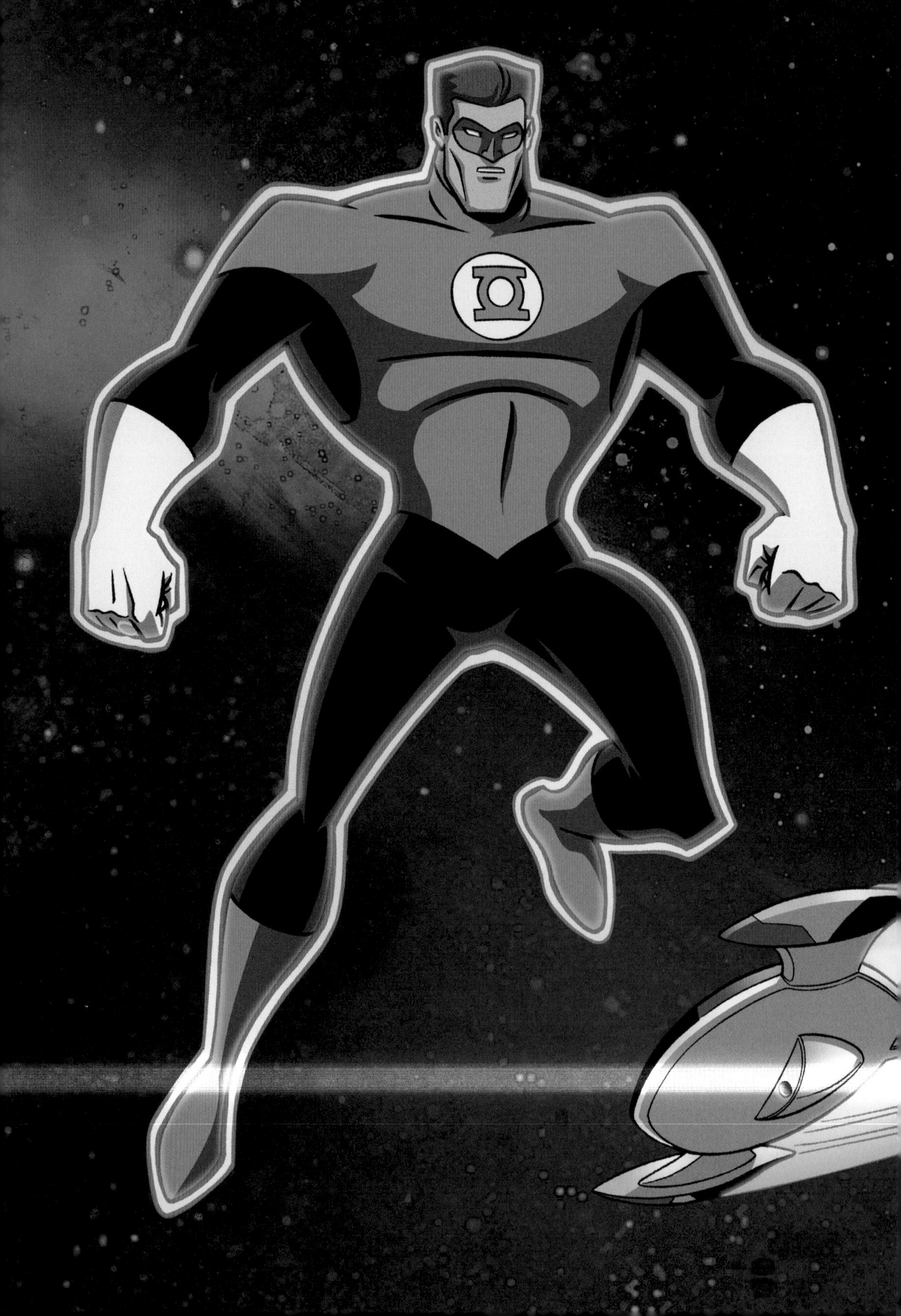

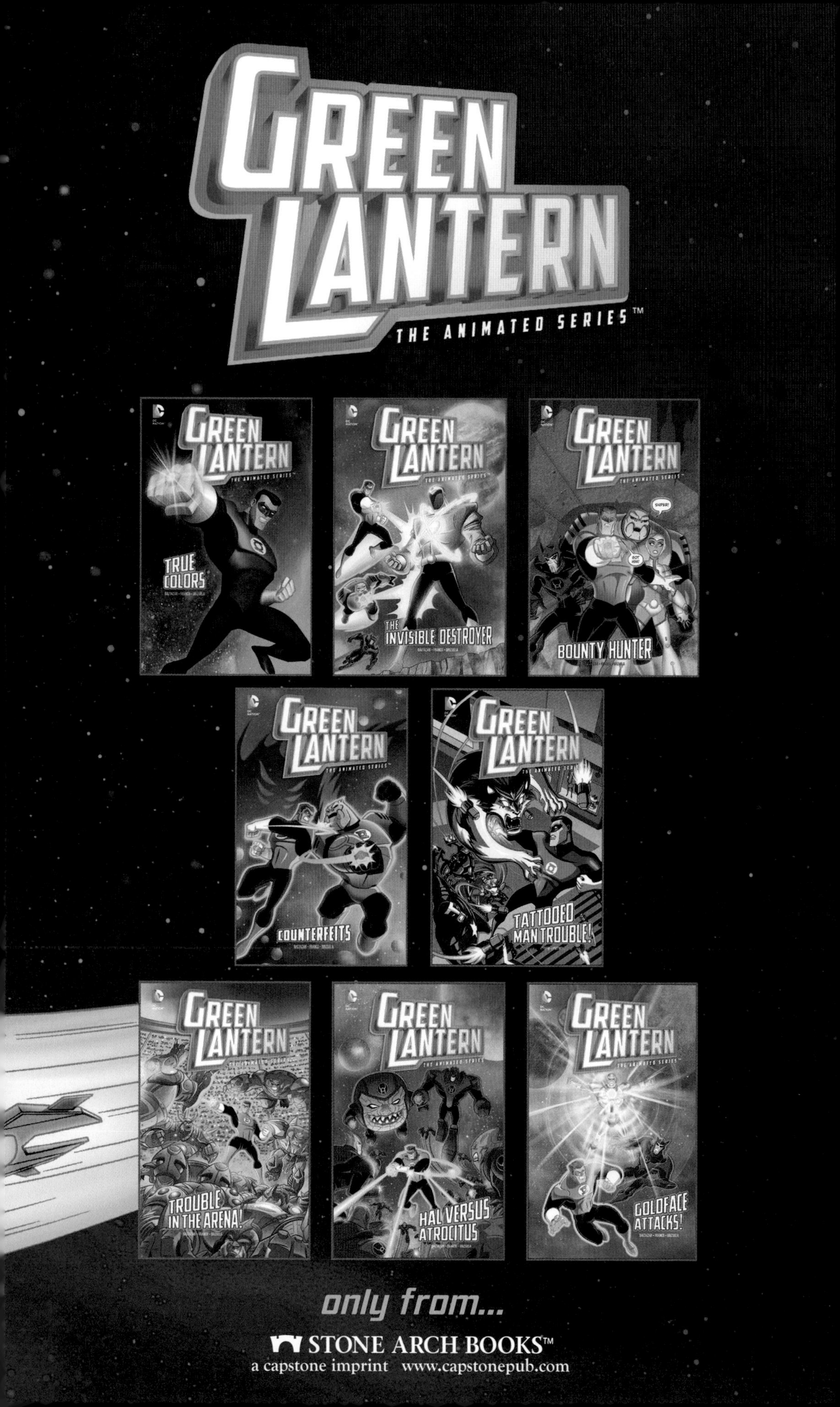
GREEN LANTERN
THE ANIMATED SERIES™
TRUE COLORS
THE INVISIBLE DESTROYER
BOUNTY HUNTER
COUNTERFEITS
TATTOOED MAN TROUBLE!
TROUBLE IN THE ARENA!
HAL VERSUS ATROCITUS
GOLDFACE ATTACKS!
only from...
STONE ARCH BOOKS™
a capstone imprint www.capstonepub.com

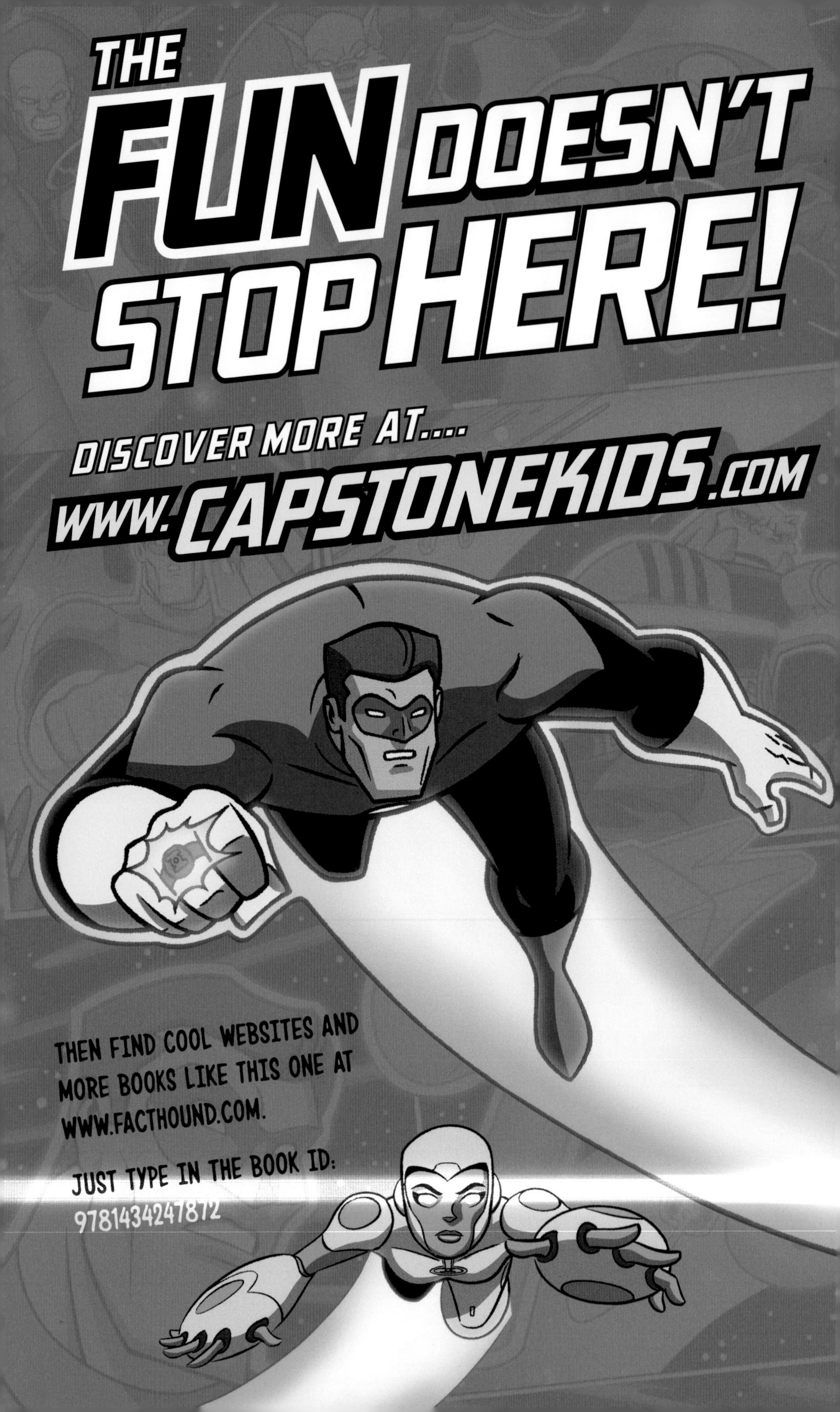
THE FUN DOESN'T STOP HERE!
DISCOVER MORE AT....
WWW.CAPSTONEKIDS.COM
THEN FIND COOL WEBSITES AND MORE BOOKS LIKE THIS ONE AT WWW.FACTHOUND.COM.
JUST TYPE IN THE BOOK ID:
9781434247872